CREED
of Redemption

S. I. N. ROCKSTAR TRILOGY

S.R. WATSON & SHAWN DAWSON

Creed of Redemption (S.I.N. Rock Star Trilogy)- Book #2
Copyright © 2016 S.R. Watson & Shawn Dawson
First Edition: August 2016

ISBN-13: 978-1536830415
ISBN-10: 1536830410

Cover Design: Sommer Stein of Perfect Pear Creative Covers (http://www.ppccovers.com)
Editor: Vanessa Leret Bridges of PREMA (https://www.premaromance.com)
Photographer: Allan Spiers of Allan Spiers Photography (http://www.allanspiers.com)
Formatter: Stacey Blake of Champagne Formats
Cover Model: Shawn Dawson (https://www.facebook.com/ShawnSDawson)

Creed of Redemption
Original Song Lyrics by Diesel

I told myself that I'd never look back

I was the reason for all your pain and I never wanted to
hurt you again

I never wanted to be the reason for your tears so it was
best that I moved on

But then you forgave me for all my past sins

You refused to give my heart back and it was then that
the road to my redemption began

Here is my creed of Redemption

I promise to be a better man this time around

My heart was never mine from the minute you came
around

Here is my creed of redemption

I will give you my all

You've seen me at my worst

You see me like nobody else can

You have my heart and I will forever be your man

Redemption

Redemption

You're my redemption

Prologue

2 Months Ago

Sevyn

THE CATASTROPHIC SCENE THAT JUST UNFOLDED BEFORE me has left me rocked. I didn't wait for Diesel to give me the green light before showing up here and now I may have ruined everything. The hurt. The disgust. The eyes never lie. Lourdes made it blatantly clear that she doesn't want to have anything to do with either of us. I watch helplessly as my brother paces frantically, running his hands through his hair. With each distraught step, I witness his regression back to a place I know well. I've seen it, so I recognize it. He hits the wall near the kitchen before resting his head on his forearm. The wall is the only thing holding him up. "Fuck this shit," he mumbles to himself a few times. The Diesel I grew up with is back, and it fucking rips my heart open. He let someone in and in its brevity, he was truly happy. Somehow Lourdes reached him—two broken pieces mended each other. Now she's gone because she feels betrayed. Thing is, Diesel was going to tell her. He just needed time. Our story is not a pleasant one. Yes, we are identical twins, but there is a reason that we are carbon copies of one another. A fucked-up reason, but necessary all the same.

I want to go to him, but I'm to blame for this. I needed to talk with him and I wasn't getting through to him on his phone. My haste has unraveled our plan. I can't even concentrate on the reason I came here in the first place. It will have to wait.

"I'm sorry, brother," I say from the sofa. I know these words are futile, but I don't know what else to say. "Tell me what I can do to fix this."

"Nothing Sevyn. There is fucking nothing you can do. You've done enough, don't you think?" Diesel hits the wall again and pieces of sheetrock crumble to the floor. "I've fucking lost her."

"Diesel—," I start, but he holds up his hand to silence me.

"Don't! It's done. This is the reason I don't fucking let anyone get close to me. You give them the power to hurt you. I won't make that mistake again." He walks over to the window with his hands still in a fist and just stares out into the distance. "I didn't deserve her anyway," he adds faintly.

I can't stand here and watch him self-destruct—become a shell of his old self. Knowing I did this is more than I can stand right now. In one instant, I've managed to wreck two people with my carelessness. I have to get the hell out of here. I can't be here for Diesel because he will not let me—not this version of him.

"I'm so sorry Diesel. Just know, you do deserve someone like Lourdes. She needs someone like you." I get up from the sofa and head toward the stairs leading to the first floor. "I'll be in touch. I hope things work themselves out. Give it time and then tell her everything. I think she will understand."

Diesel turns to face me now. "What did you come for? What did you have to tell me that was so important that it couldn't have fucking waited until I called you back?"

"Nothing that can't wait now. I should've just waited. I know I fucked up," I retort.

Diesel closes the distance between us in a blur. He's nearly nose to nose with me now. "Are you serious right now? You just turned my damn world upside down and now you want to leave without giving me an explanation as to why? Think again, *brother.*" His nostrils flare, and I know he is restraining himself from pummeling the shit out of me.

"It's about our father," I start.

"Your father, but continue," he corrects. He is wound tight. His body is stiff and those fists are at his side, ready to engage.

"He's dying!" I blurt out. I watch as the wind is knocked from his sails with that piece of news. His face falls before he works to school his features.

"Good. At least one good thing came out of this fucking disastrous day." His shoulders drop and his fists loosen. His words are at odds with how he looks. He looks lost and I don't know how to fix it. I know he doesn't mean what he just said. He has every reason to hate our father, yet in this moment, I'm not so sure that he does, despite his vile words.

He turns on his heel and heads upstairs to the third

floor. Our conversation is over.

I'll go for now. He needs time to digest this news and work his shit out with Lourdes. Our plan can wait. As I walk through the bushes to the motorcycle I have hidden, guilt gnaws at me. Thing is, I had an instant connection with Lourdes. I look toward the docks and I remember the first time I saw her there. Everyone was out enjoying the lake and she just sat there in the fucking August heat in baggy ass jeans and a black t-shirt. I shouldn't have been attracted to her, but I was. Something about her intrigued me. Then she opened her mouth and her sass pulled me in further. Diesel had already warned me about their little spat so I would be armed with the info I needed to double as him, but I didn't care. I wasn't going to let her stay mad. I didn't change out of my clothes either. I sat my ass on that hot fucking dock with her and was determined to see her smile.

I knew she could never be mine, but each time I doubled as Diesel in the house, my will was tested. Together Diesel and I had a plan and she wasn't part of it. When Diesel fell for her, I knew I needed to close the door on the possibility of Lourdes and me. I know what my brother is feeling as far as Lourdes is concerned because, sadly, I feel it too. I wanted to run after her just as much as he did. She managed to get through to both of us and now she's gone. Now I don't have to pretend—to keep my feelings to myself. I should be relieved, but instead, I hate that I squandered a chance at happiness for my brother. I really do hope they work it out, even at the expense of my own happiness.

CHAPTER
One

Lourdes

I STARE INTO THE FULL-LENGTH MIRROR IN THE DORM room that I used to share with Brooke. The spring semester here at University of Alabama starts in a few days, yet all of my classes are online. I stare at the reflection of the dumbass looking back at me in the mirror, who might be about to make yet another mistake she'll regret. I can't believe I agreed to go on tour with Sex in Numbers. When I walked—no, when I stormed—away from the lake house two months ago, I swore I would never see Diesel or his twin brother ever again. Diesel nearly destroyed me. He let me fall for him while he and his twin brother substituted in and out of my life at their fucking convenience. Was any of it real? Hell, I don't even know who my feelings were for.

I desperately wanted to escape Alabama in that moment, but my life was here now. I had school obligations, not to mention, I was in Brooke's car at the time. These things kept me from running, but it was Brooke who helped me keep my sanity. She wouldn't let me go back to being the insecure girl who hid behind dark makeup and baggy clothes. Every day was a struggle to just exist, but I took it one day at a time. Although I still hurt, the pain fades a little more with each passing day.

"Are you having second thoughts?" Brooke asks as she comes in and catches me staring blankly at myself in the mirror.

"Well, it's not like I'm anxious to be around Diesel again. That part sucks, but this is not for him. I can't let him fuck up this opportunity for me." Brooke nods approvingly.

"Smart girl," she replies. *I'm glad somebody thinks so.*

Xander invited me last month to join their tour for a month or so. He thought it would be a great experience to continue documenting their journey. This is a valuable opportunity for my aspirations as music journalist. My peers would kill for the chance. Textbooks and the classroom can only teach so much. Because of this, I told him I would think it over. Xander never found out about my brief fling with Diesel, if you can call it that. He would have kicked his ass and the band's dream of a record deal, would have probably been over before it started. No, Diesel came clean about who Sevyn was and left the explanation at that. He never told the guys that he and his brother exchanged places in the house, who knows how many times. He simply told the guys he had a twin

6

brother but that it couldn't be made public due to personal reasons. Nobody outside the band was allowed to know. The guys all respected his need for privacy, especially since it was Sevyn that connected them with Desiree. Of course, Xander wanted to keep me in the loop so he told me, after swearing me to secrecy. If he only knew how I really found out. I stayed quiet for the sake of keeping the band intact.

Surprisingly, it was Brooke who talked me into saying yes to joining Xander on the tour. She pointed out that I didn't have to stay the entire time. I only needed to stay long enough to get the gist of life behind the scenes. She pleaded with me to not let Diesel ruin this for me.

"I like this strong woman standing here next to me," she continues. I snap out of my reverie. I don't know how strong I am, but we're about to see.

"We'll see" I begin. "Besides, it will give me a chance to get to know Lily. She and Xander are getting kind of serious I think. He didn't tell me this, but he asked her to join him on tour as well. That's huge!"

"Yeah, it is. It means no groupie pussy for him," Brooke snickers. I don't want to even think about seeing Diesel with all the groupies. I just have to keep telling myself that chapter of my life is closed.

"Xander's not like that anyway. He's always been a one woman kind of guy. At least from what I've seen." They do call themselves Sex in Numbers, so who knows. I've never witnessed him having player tendencies so that's all that matters.

"Wish more men were like him," Brooke huffs. Most guys just want to see how many bitches they can bang.

"What about Mike?" We met James and Mike at the club

while the guys were performing one night. She and Mike have been seeing each other for about three months, which is a change for Brooke. She doesn't normally keep the same guy around long. She gets bored with them quick.

"Oh, I'm sure he's a dog like the rest of them. He just hasn't shown his true colors yet. I have my eye on him, though. Any sign of bullshit and his ass will get benched," she winks.

"You can't look for stuff woman. Give the guy a chance." Fancy me trying to give someone relationship advice. I couldn't even sniff out I was being played. Whatever, we can't both be pessimistic.

"Come on, girlie. We can't just stand here talking about these guys. You have a bus to get on tomorrow, and we have some shopping to do before then." She's already grabbing her purse off the bed.

"I do need to get a few things," I agree.

"Girl, you are going to be on tour with some hot-as-fuck men. I'm sure you'll get to go to some awesome celebrity parties and meet some new prospects. We can't have you looking plain Jane," she says with a giggle. "Just so you know, every break I get, I'm joining you. I'm inviting myself." We both laugh, but I know she isn't kidding.

"I like plain Jane," I tease. "It's better than being skanky. There will be enough of that, I'm sure."

"True. Okay, we'll find you a happy medium somewhere in the middle. Now come on, woman," she says, pushing me out the door.

DIESEL

I take in the sweetness of this bus and I feel like I need to pinch myself. Desiree didn't spare no expenses. We're hitting the road in style. It's like we have a luxury hotel on wheels.

"I take it you like?" Desiree appears behind me. I've been so busy checking out all the cool features of the bus that I didn't even hear her get on. The guys are outside loading the last of their equipment and waiting for Lourdes to arrive.

"Hell yeah, I do!" I grin. "But can we afford all of this? This fucker is huge." I don't even want to think about what this is hitting us for.

"The tour is sold out. You guys touring with Reckless Ambition is the best move we could have made to get your name out there. Trust me. You guys can afford this and if everything works out as planned, you all will be climbing the charts in no time."

Reckless Ambition is the rock band that we will be opening for. They are killing the Billboard charts right now. Desiree is definitely impressing me. I have no doubt that she will help get us to the top.

"I'm looking forward to it." She puts a hand on her hip and my eyes follow. She always wears these sexy pantsuits that make it impossible for a man not to appreciate her curves. She clears her throat, and I know I've been busted.

"Your first stop is in Los Angeles, so you guys will have a long drive ahead from Alabama. You'll get there in time to rehearse before your first show, though. You'll also meet Ivy and the guys at that time. I'm flying there, so I'll see you guys in a few days."

"We'll be ready. I'm glad there is an area set aside for us to rehearse. I swear everything we could possibly need has been thought of."

"Yeah, I might have added some specifications for them to include," she smiles. "Just make sure you and the guys behave. Ivy is off limits. Don't fuck this up." Before I can respond, she waves me off and heads off the bus.

Ivy performs backup vocals for Reckless Ambition, and she is the fucking epitome of sexy. She has short, red hair and green eyes that pierce through you. She has a tattoo sleeve on her right arm and perky little tits that make every dick within a mile radius stand at attention. Not to mention, her vocals are the shit. Desiree has every right to put that warning on the table, but I don't really have any plans to smash that. That's like shitting where you sleep. My three fuck rule has been back in full force since my incident with Lourdes.

I broke her. Not intentionally, but it doesn't matter. Shit was better when I stuck to my rules. Now that I'll be on the road, one night stands are all that I can offer. It's better this way. No attachments or expectations. It's been two months since I've seen or talked with Lourdes. We never made contact after that day she walked in on me and Sevyn. I tried to call and apologize a few times before I finally gave up. She needed to move on—to heal. I was surprised when Xander proposed that she join us on the tour for a bit. He thought it would be a good experience for her music journalist major and a bonus for Lily, since he had already invited her too. How in the hell could I object to that when the rest of the guys were okay with it? I would look like the biggest jerk! I finally came clean, letting them know I had been hiding the fact that I had a twin, and that was enough so I just kept my opinions to myself.

I'm going to be me. I'm going to fuck bitches and I can't be worried about Lourdes's feelings. Truth is, her leaving the way she did hurt me too. I fucking opened up to her—broke all my rules for her—and in the end, she didn't give me the benefit of the doubt. She didn't give me a chance to explain or fix it. It wasn't easy to let her in, and I did. She made me feel again and then ripped my damn heart open. No woman will ever get that chance again. The last two months have been hell. I didn't stop until I fucked her out of my system and I have no intentions of going back down that road, so I hope she has moved on like I have.

My thoughts are interrupted by the Honda Accord pulling into the driveway. She's here. She gets out of the car, and the feelings that rush through me are indescribable. I'm glad I'm alone on the bus so I can get a good look at her. Her waist-length hair is brown now—I'm guessing it's her natural color. I prefer brunettes anyway. She is wearing fitted jeans that make her ass look even more perfect. It makes me think of the last time I was balls deep in her tight pussy while my hand gripped her delectable round ass. *Fuck!* I can't let my thoughts go there. It was so easy to put her out of mind when I didn't have to see her. She's no longer mine. I need to get a fucking grip. We need to hurry and get this bus moving. The sooner I can get my dick into some new pussy, the better.

Lourdes

I hug Brooke goodbye while the guys take my suitcases aboard the bus. I don't see Diesel yet, but I need to prepare myself. I don't know what to expect. The guys don't know we once had a thing, so how should we act around each other?

"You be strong," Brooke whispers. "And you better call me."

"I will," I promise.

"Okay, go already before I cry," she sniffles. "I'll be at boring college parties while you're living it up with celebrities." She jokes, but I can tell she really is sad to see me go.

"Hush. You love the frat parties. Besides, you'll be joining us when you get a break. I'll call you every day."

"Sure you will," she teases. "Okay, I'm really going now. I'm sure the guys are ready to get going."

I turn to see that everyone has boarded the bus. I hug her one more time before I let her go. I can already tell this is going to be harder than I thought.

Trepidation gnaws at me as I step onto the bus, but I plaster a smile on my face. "Sorry guys! I didn't mean to hold you up."

"Nonsense. Get over here," Xander says pulling me into a hug.

"Nice to see you again, princess," Keyser and Gable mock. I forgot all about that stupid nickname. It had a different ring to it coming from Diesel though. I look over at him and he gives me a subtle chin lift as a way of hello. Our eyes lock for the briefest of seconds before he returns attention to his phone. His hair has grown out some and he's even sexier than I remember.

"Where's Lily?" I ask. I need to keep my thoughts away from Diesel.

"She is in one of the bunks taking a nap," Xander explains. "Come, let me show you to your bunk." I follow behind him while taking in the opulence of everything. This bus is gorgeous—definitely quite a few classes above our dorm room.

"Wow, this is a lot of space," I gasp. There are two sets of bunks side by side, with another set directly across for a total of eight bunks. They even have little TVs in each one.

"Yeah. They are twin size. There is a master bedroom toward the back of the bus and that is where some of our luggage is kept. The rest is stored underneath the bus. We decided it would be fair if we didn't appoint one person to get the bedroom. Instead, we'll use it to rehearse—,"

"And as the designated fuck room," Diesel adds, cutting Xander off.

He drops that bomb and walks right past us to his bunk. Apparently, his is on top of mine. *Great.*

"Shut it, Diesel. Have some respect, man!" Xander chastises.

"Might as well open her eyes now, bro. You're the one who invited her to tag along. This isn't a daycare. We won't be filtering what we say. At least I won't."

"I didn't ask you to, jack ass!" How dare he? That tag along jab stung, but I'll be damned if I let it show. It's apparent he doesn't want me here. *Noted.*

"Don't be a fucking tool, Diesel." Xander glares at him,

and the tension between the two is palpable. This is what I don't want.

"Whatever," Diesel dismisses. He reaches up and grabs the earphones from his bunk and leaves without another word.

"I'm so sorry, Lourdes," Xander starts.

"It's not a big deal. I halfway know what to expect and it doesn't bother me. I don't want you guys to be anyone other than yourselves. I'm documenting the band's music journey, so I sure as hell don't want a scripted one." He shakes his head, but I can tell he is starting to calm down. "It'll be okay. Promise me that you won't give me any special treatment."

"Lourdes—," he tries to object.

"Promise, Xander, or I'll have them turn this bus around and take me back. That's not what I'm here for."

"Fine, princess. I know you have to experience it all. It's just, to me, you're still my baby sister. I respect what you're asking so I promise to lay off." He pulls me into a hug.

"Thank you."

"Of course. Just know the bedroom is open to anyone when we're not rehearsing. If you want to go in there for a nap, just to get away from the testosterone for bit, or just whatever. It has a bigger walk-in shower in the master bath too. The smaller one is toward the front of the bus."

Xander grabs my hand to show me the room. Just wow. This bedroom is so luxurious. The bed looks so plush. I just want to get lost in that thread count. Oh and the mirrors. They're everywhere. I bet some kinky shit will go down in here. My heart sinks a little when I think about that kinky shit being with Diesel.

"It's really nice Xander," I muster without tearing up.

"Mhmm. Desiree did a good job. She got this bus for us." He beams with pride. "You should check out the glass shower and jacuzzi tub in here."

"Maybe another time. A nap really does sound good right now. Brooke and I were up half the night talking, getting our last bit of girl time in before I left." This all feels overwhelming all of a sudden. I'm both excited, and scared shitless. I can feel my unresolved feelings for Diesel trying to resurrect themselves and he's made it clear that he has moved on. He's already counting down the time until he can use that bedroom. I'll never sleep in there and I don't know how to prepare myself to listen to him fucking someone else. My bunk is close to the master bedroom, so hearing what goes down in there is inevitable. I remember how much it hurt that day when I realized he fucked Brooke's cousin, Sasha. I didn't have to listen to it, it was enough just to know she had a piece of him. We weren't even in a relationship at the time. This is a fucking disaster waiting to happen, and I have no choice but to watch it play out. He's no longer mine.

CHAPTER

Two

DIESEL

W E'VE BEEN ON THE ROAD TWO HOURS NOW, BUT Lourdes still hasn't come out from her bunk to join us. Who knows if she's still napping. I know I was somewhat of an insensitive douche earlier, but I had to set the tone. If she had any doubts about things remaining between us or rekindling what we had, I had to nip that shit in the bud. I'm not going back to that being that man she once knew. She wanted to join us so she will have to get used to seeing me fuck other bitches.

The guys are already drinking beers to celebrate our new beginning. Even Lily has a beer. She's sitting on Xander's lap and it's pretty evident that he's pussy whipped. There will be no groupie ass for him—oh well, more for me. They're being so loud, nobody notices when Lourdes comes into the room wiping her eyes. *Holy fuck*! My dick stands at complete attention in a nanosecond. She's wearing some skimpy fucking black gym shorts that barely cover the bottom of her ass cheeks. With her arms raised to wipe the sleep from her eyes, a hint of silver jewelry sparkles from her navel. When the fuck did she get that?

"You guys are loud," she says groggily. You can hear a pin drop now. With the exception of Xander, I know every motherfucker in here just popped a boner. That petite waist and curvaceous ass are beckoning me to pull her in that room and be the first to christen that fucking bed.

"Uh, Lourdes. Where are your clothes, princess?" Xander is trying to be sweet about it, but I know he can see the lust in our eyes. I hate that they're seeing what I'm seeing, but she's not mine.

"Hush, Xander. These are clothes," she says pulling her tank back down over her belly. Only now, her fucking tits bulge over the top and I can't say shit.

"I'm going to go ask Stewart how far we are from the next town. I'm starving," I say as an excuse to get the hell away from her. I'm starving, all right. I want to suck and tease those fucking tits of hers while I pound the shit out of her. Seems my dick hasn't gotten the memo that her three fuck limit is more than over. I get up and excuse myself after I get my dick under control.

"Tell him we want pizza," I hear Gable shout behind me.

If they wanted pizza, they should have been the one going to talk to Stewart. I need to get back on my meal plan. We need to get groceries on this bus. These shit heads are not going to make me fuck off my diet. No, I'll be cooking tonight. Stewart agrees to stop within an hour in Mississippi.

"So are we getting pizza?" Keyser asks from the card table when I get back. I can barely concentrate, though. Lourdes is sitting on the sofa directly across from where I was originally sitting. She has one leg resting on the floor and the other resting on the sofa. I can see up her shorts. The crease of where her pussy and leg meet is fucking taunting me. I can almost see the outline. She sees me looking and puts the other leg on the sofa so I can get a perfect impression of her pussy lips through her flimsy ass shorts.

Thank God the guys don't notice. They've all headed to the table to play Spades. Lourdes is playing a dangerous game with me. There's no way in hell she doesn't know what she's doing. This is not the same shy girl I met in the fall. She got her bellybutton pierced, she's wearing skimpy as fuck clothes, and she is willingly showing me her pussy? Who the hell is this woman who boarded this bus with us? I don't know how to feel about this change. I know it's no longer my concern, but fuck, fuck, fuck!

"What the hell, man? Are we getting pizza or not?" Keyser yells across the room.

"Uh no," I say trying to regain my wits. "We're going to stop at a grocery store so we don't have to keep stopping for food. I'll cook tonight."

"Ah, hell. We're going to be stuck on this bus with Diesel's healthy ass food," Xander teases. The guys let out a collective groan and Lily giggles.

"Shut up, asswipes. How long have I been enduring the

shit you all call food? Keep it up and I won't buy alcohol either. We can all start fresh." I know they would never go for that, but it's fun to watch them shoot me the finger.

"Lourdes and I will eat healthy with you, won't we Lourdes?" Lily laughs even harder. "We have to watch our girlish figures," she continues. Lourdes gives me a thumbs up. I know Lily is only joking since neither of them have issues in that department. Hell, I'm watching Lourdes's figure right now.

"Baby, you are perfect just the way you are," Xander says to Lily. We all make gagging noises except Lourdes.

The bus starts to slow so I look out the window. We're pulling into the lot of a grocery store. Lourdes follows my gaze and then jumps up.

"I'll grab my flip flops," she announces. "I'm coming in too. I have a few things I forgot to get."

"You need more than shoes if you're fucking coming into the store with me," I growl. I'm not going to watch the whole store ogle her ass.

"You're not the boss of me Diesel," she smarts off.

"Fine! Stay on the bus then." I don't have time for this shit. As soon as the bus comes to a complete stop, I'm out. I head straight back to the meat department. Shit, I forgot the list I made. Lourdes is already driving me crazy. I pick through a few packs of chicken breast until I find the ones I want. I hate shopping in stores that I'm unfamiliar with because I hate searching for shit. My shit is always on the outer aisles since I eat fresh, but it's hell searching for the shit I know the guys like. I run into Keyser in the frozen food section.

"What? I'm getting the frozen pizza," he chuckles. "Everybody got off because they all had something they needed to get. I think it's disorganized as fuck, but nobody made a list so whatever." I keep quiet about my list. He said everybody got off the bus. That means Lourdes is around here somewhere in those fuck me shorts.

I don't have to wonder long. My trip to find the shampoo has me in direct line of sight with her bending over to read a bottle of Nexxus. Before she knows it, I'm on her. I spin her so that her back is against the shelves. Several bottles of shampoo topple over, but I don't give a shit.

"What the fuck are you trying to do to me, Lourdes?" My hands grip her thighs. That's not where they want to be, though.

"I'm not trying to do shit to you," she says breathily. "Get off me." She's spitting mad yet she doesn't do a very good job of trying to convince me she wants me to let her go. My hands curve around her ass as I pull her into me. I want her to feel how hard she is making my dick. Maybe I should just fuck her once to stave off the itch.

"Why did you show me your pussy on the bus then? Why are you being a cock tease if you're not dying for me to fuck you?" Her chest heaves, and I watch her tits rub against me. I want to slide my fingers inside her shorts and feel just how wet she is for me. My mouth is inches from hers now. I just need a taste.

"I thought I was putting on a show for Sevyn," she whispers against my lips. I fucking freeze. It's like she's just thrown a bucket of ice water on me. That was a low blow. One I didn't think she was capable of.

"What? You know I have difficulty telling you guys apart," she jabs. I release her immediately. I want to fucking punch something, but instead I swipe a row of shampoo off the shelf. She wants my fucking brother? Well, fuck her. I can't even look at her right now.

"Diesel," she squeals over the mess I made.

"Stay the fuck away from me, Lourdes!" I don't even get what I came down this aisle for. I make a beeline for the register to check out. Thankfully, I'm the first one back on the bus. I need a moment to regain my composure. I bring all my stuff in and leave it on the counter. I head to the master bedroom and lock the door. The urge to fucking punch something is still strong, so I start the shower and let it get hot before I get in. I angrily stroke my dick as the water rains down on me. I'm furious that Lourdes has me feeling this way. I hate that she can still get under my skin. I pump my dick faster, hoping that each stroke rids me of my desire for her. Only when I finally come, it ignites my anger even more. I get too much pussy to jerk off. *Fuck her, goddamn it!*

I hear someone beating on the bedroom door. "Diesel, open up man." I recognize the voice to belong to Keyser, yelling.

I get out of the shower and towel myself dry. I wrap the towel around me before I walk into the bedroom and open the door. "What the hell Keyser?"

"You just disappeared. I came to check on you." He looks genuinely concerned. He must sense that something is up.

"I just wanted some privacy to have a shower before everybody got back on the bus. Why are you being weird?" He looks relieved.

"Makes sense. I wish I would have thought of that actually," he laughs. He shakes his head, feeling foolish. "I just need to make sure I get my shower before the women do. They can spend an eternity in here. Especially in that tub."

"Yeah, well let me change and it's all yours. I'll make dinner when I come out." That seems to satisfy him.

"Okay. I'll put the groceries away then." He walks off. I don't even bother telling him to wait until I pull out what I'm going to cook. I just close the door and fall back on the bed. I'll get dressed in a minute.

I don't know how long I'm out for. I awake to pitch blackness and the bus moving. I stumble around until I finally find the light switch. I grab my phone off the dresser and see that a couple of hours have passed. I guess I was more tired than I thought. That and busting that nut didn't help. It was over after that. Shit. Now, I'm late starting dinner. Those fuckers probably already baked the pizza. I find my duffle bag and just throw on a pair of basketball shorts. The minute I walk out of the room, an aroma of herbs and spices tantalizes my senses. It smells so damn good.

Lily and Lourdes are in the kitchen cooking. I see that Lily is making a spinach salad with strawberries and walnuts. Lourdes's back is still to me as she pulls chicken breast from the oven. She is bending over again and flashbacks from the scene earlier come rushing to my mind. *Fuck me.* I divert my attention to the guys sitting at the table across from the kitchen.

"You guys are actually eating healthy?" I chuckle. "Sorry, I crashed. I just knew your asses would have gone for the pizza."

"Oh, believe me, we wanted to, but the women said no. They knew you were set on eating something healthy so they volunteered to cook so you could sleep," Gable admits.

"Yeah, we were outnumbered." Keyser grins. I can't help laughing now.

"How were you outnumbered, dipshit? That's two against three or three against three if you count my vote."

"Whatever. You get your damn healthy meal, while we eat like birds. You know Xander is pussy whipped so his vote is whatever Lily's is. That makes it three against two." He has a point there.

"Hey," Xander objects. We ignore him.

"I'm going to eat that shit with my beer," Gable chimes in. We all laugh at the banter we have going on while the women give us evil stares from the kitchen.

"Did I just hear you call our food shit?" Lily asks in mock exasperation.

"Don't pay them no mind, babe," Xander says going to her side. He leans down and gives her a kiss. I want to barf. Those two are nauseatingly sweet. I'm glad he's happy though. I catch a glimpse of Lourdes looking at them longingly. She turns back toward the stove and begins putting the chicken on plates.

"Is there something I can help with?" I ask. I'm not a complete ass. I appreciate that they cooked and let me sleep.

"No, I think we got it," Lourdes says softly. The sass from earlier has disappeared. I step aside and let her arrange the food to be served. The guys waste no time grabbing a plate as soon as they're given the go ahead. They talked all that noise about my healthy food and now they're rushing into the kitchen. It's quite comical.

Lourdes doesn't grab a plate for herself though. Instead she heads toward the back of the bus.

"You're not eating?" Xander questions before she gets too far.

"No. I nibbled while we were cooking. I'm going to go grab a shower."

"Oh. Okay then," Xander replies. I look over at Keyser. I wonder if he ever got his shower after I knocked the hell out. I know he wanted to get in there before the women. His eyes meet mine and he answers my unasked question by giving me a thumbs up. I must have really been out because I sure as hell didn't hear him in there.

We all finish our food in record time. Xander volunteers to put everything away and load the dishwasher. I know we're going to have to come up with some kind of chore schedule so this place doesn't become a pigsty, but for tonight, I'm just glad it isn't me. While everyone heads to the card table to resume their game of Spades, I opt for some alone time in my bunk. I grab a pen and paper from my bag. I have a song I've been working on that I haven't told the guys about because I'm not sure if I want it produced or not, yet. I started this song when Lourdes walked out of my life. The lyrics make me feel vulnerable. I don't know if I want to share that. It was around the same time that Sevyn dropped the news that his father was dying. They don't know how much time he has left. He hasn't come clean about his health with his investors or shareholders. From what Sevyn tells me, he's trying to get his affairs in order and ensure that Sevyn is in a position to take over after he's gone.

Whatever, Claude has been dead to me since high school, and me to him. I don't want to give him another thought. I have so much shit built up inside. My lyrics are my outlet— my release. Some of these songs will never be shared. They're mine. It's part of the reason why my process is so private. The guys don't necessarily understand it, but they respect it. It works for us. I give them the lyrics that I want to share and then help lay tracks to it. I haven't touched this one particular song in a few weeks, but now that Lourdes is back in my life, the words are flowing. I have to get them down on paper. I can't go back to her, though, so the quicker we get off this bus and I get some action, the better. The temptation is just too great—too real.

CHAPTER
Three

Lourdes

THE SMELL OF EGGS WAKES ME BEFORE MY ALARM. I'D set it last night so that I could get up and jot some notes about their experience so far. I had an idea to write a book about their journey, if it's okay with the group. I'll talk with the guys later today to see if they'll give their permission. I don't know why I didn't think of this before. I have no doubt that these guys are going to be famous once the world has a chance to hear them. I would have an exclusive look into how their life as rock stars started from the beginning. I'm super giddy at the prospect. I just hope they say yes.

I ease from my bunk and note that Diesel's bunk above mine is empty. Maybe he slept in the bedroom. The moment

I step into the kitchen, my ovaries damn near combust. Diesel is making omelets, wearing nothing but pajama bottoms that are hanging dangerously low. The corded muscles of his back flex with each flip of the egg. I'm guessing he can feel my presence, because he turns and catches me staring. I can see the imprint of his cock as it moves against the cotton fabric. I will my eyes to look up, but then his abs hypnotize me even more.

"Are you hungry? Hello?" He waves his hand to get my attention and I snap out of my lustful trance. Apparently he has been trying to get my attention, but I was too busy enjoying the view. *Nice. I've been busted.* "Well?"

"Well what?" I ask flustered. I walk the remaining way into the kitchen to see what k-cups they have for the Keurig. I need coffee.

"I asked if you were hungry. I have egg white omelets with just veggies or you can have the one with the works to clog your arteries. Pick your poison," he says jokingly. I'm glad that things are light between us this morning. I was sure our store scene would set us back to not even being friends. I don't even know why I threw Sevyn in his face. He was being all flirty and making me feel things that I'm not supposed to feel. I have forgiven him, but I won't forget—I won't get caught up with him again. I was mad that he made me want him so I lashed out.

"I'm sorry about what I said to you in the store yesterday, Diesel. I knew you weren't Sevyn. It's just you were coming on strong and I didn't want that."

"Old news, *princess!*" I laugh because his use of my nickname doesn't sounds as condescending as it did last time.

"What's so funny?" He pours orange juice into a carafe.

"Nothing. Look, I don't want to fight. You guys have a forty-show tour over the next four months. I just want to keep the peace."

"You're staying the entire four months?" He looks surprised. "I thought you were only sticking around for a month tops."

"Xander—that sneaky bastard," I hear him murmur to himself.

"That was the plan. I just decided last night I wanted to stick around. I have a proposal for the band."

"Shoot," he encourages.

"Um, I kind of wanted to wait and talk to everybody," I say hesitantly.

"You need to understand the hierarchy around here, Lourdes. I'm the primary decision maker for the band."

"I thought that was Desiree's job," I retort. I feel our easy vibe this morning slipping away as his jerk tendencies threaten to emerge.

"Calm your tits, princess. Don't be cute," he says defensively. "She's our manager, true. She's the liaison between us and the label, but I still speak for the group."

"Wow. Does anybody else get a say? Sounds pretty narcissistic if you ask me," I push.

"Well, nobody asked you. You're the one that has something to ask of us. I decide what to take to the group and then we vote as a band. It's my fucking duty to look out for us and filter unnecessary bullshit. It's worked for us thus far. You're getting into something that is not you're business. Either tell me what you want or don't. I'm going to eat my damn omelet before it gets cold. He grabs a plate and leaves me standing in the kitchen so I follow him.

"Okay. I don't want to get into the whole group dynamic thing, so if I need to present my idea to you, so be it."

He takes a seat at the table, and I slide in next to him.

"I want to write a book," I rush out. "About the band."

"What about us? We really don't need our personal shit exploited," he grumbles as he eats his eggs.

"I'm not interested in doing a tell-all, Diesel. It won't be anything scandalous. It would be more of a rags-to-riches kind of story. The highs, the lows, and the in between. How you guys started, what gigs you initially took, how you were discovered. That type of thing. Rehearsing on the road, the glamorous, and the not-so-glamorous part about your lives on the road, even though this bus is pretty spectacular, you get my point. You guys will have input on the story of your band." I entwine my fingers as I wait for him to shut me down again.

"Fine, but we get to read it before you publish that shit and anything that we feel would taint our image will get thrown out. Capisce?"

"Agreed," I say ecstatically.

"Don't get too excited," he warns. "I only agreed to bring your idea to the guys for a vote. They still need to say yes."

"Of course." I think the hardest part is over. I don't see the guys voting against Diesel if he is okay with it. Now to tell Brooke that I won't be back in a month, but if all goes as planned, I will have my very first book written at the end of the tour. This is the happiest I've been in a while.

Within the next hour, they guys finally begin to emerge

from their bunks. They must have had a late night. I was in bed before nine. I wait until they've all grabbed a plate and, more importantly, a cup of coffee. The same coffee that I forgot to make apparently. My stomach growls, reminding me that I need to eat. I haven't eaten yet. I'm too nervous and too excited.

"Guys, Lourdes has an idea she would like to propose," Diesel says suddenly when everyone is sitting around the table. A lump the size of a golf ball swells in my throat. What if they say no?

"Spill it already, Lourdes. Your pacing is going to giving me motion sickness," Xander jokes. Everybody laughs and I can feel the tension release. I give my spiel like word vomit. I just want to get the idea out there so I can run and hide.

"Hmm. I think you're on to something there, sis. Not to mention, once we get big, readers will be clamoring to get their hands on it." I hadn't really thought that far.

"Really wasn't thinking about turning a profit. I just think it would be great for school. I'm sure a firsthand knowledge book will go over really well in future classes."

"Nonsense. You have to always consider your return on an investment. From the time you take to write this book, to the money it will cost to get it published—it's all worth something," he assures. "I'm completely fine with it. What do you guys say?"

"Just don't put my body count in there, and we're golden," Keyser teases

"Body count?" From the three heads Diesel just spouted, I'm sure that was a dumb question.

"The number of women he's bedded," Xander clarifies as

he shakes his head.

"No, it's the number of women he's fucked or will fuck," Diesel reiterates. He throws his head back in laughter. "Xander, stop trying to sugar coat shit for your sister. She is a grown ass woman. She should know what a body count is. Stop going all *Pride and Prejudice* on us, Mr. Darcy."

"I don't care to know that tidbit anyway," I assure. "Just *ewww*."

A smile breaks across my lips. Diesel's reference to the classic book written by Jane Austen is pretty clever. I don't remember if she used words like bedded in the book, but it's funny as shit all the same. I can't hold it in anymore. I double over in laughter. Soon everyone is in hysterics. Lily walks in with a puzzled look on her face. I guess our loudness woke her up.

"Morning, everyone. Hmmm something smells heavenly," she says walking toward the kitchen.

"Diesel made omelets for everyone," I say as I get up to join her. I think I'll eat now. And make that coffee I was originally going to make. I fill Lily in on my book idea while I look through the k-cups. I find the last Starbucks Vanilla Blonde one, while making a mental note to get more the next time we stop at a store.

"That's a brilliant idea, Lourdes. Way to go girl," Lily says, congratulating me. "If you're staying, maybe I'll stick around a bit, too." Lily is also taking a couple classes online. Thank goodness for the advancement of technology and that you can pay for your own Wi-Fi through your cell phone. Not sure if they have Wi-Fi on this bus, but it seems to have everything else. It would be sweet if it did.

"Thank you." I smile. "And it would be great to have a female here with me if you could stay," I add

"I don't see why not. My parents think I'm still in the dorms anyway," Lily admits. "But don't tell Xander. I don't want him to feel bad. My parents are just a little uptight when it comes to these types of things."

"Your secret is safe will me. What parent would want to hear that their precious daughter has left school to travel with a rock band? A band that calls themselves Sex in Numbers, no less." I laugh.

"True," she states and joins in on my laughter. Lily is a pretty cool girl. She could never takes Brooke's place, but it's nice that I don't have to do all this without female company. We joke about strict parents, but truthfully, I wish my mother were still here. I wish I knew who my father was. I'm sure my mother wouldn't have be too keen on the idea of me being on the road with a band either, but then again, I have Xander.

Lily and I get lost in our own conversation, electing to just eat our breakfast in here. We compare classes, goals, and what we think this tour will be like. We should be pulling into Los Angeles by later tonight. The tour starts on the west coast with travel toward the east over the next four months. The guys will perform ten concerts a month with two to three concerts a week. I still can't believe the whole tour is sold out already.

After breakfast, the guys head toward the bedroom to rehearse. There is a spot on the bus for them to work on their music that is a bit more formal, but they choose the bedroom anyway. Lily and I shooed them off and let them know we'd get the dishes. So far so good. Diesel and I seem to have mended some of our wounds and the overall atmosphere is relaxed. I suspect things will change once the concerts start, but for now, I'll enjoy the reprieve.

Two days on this bus and I'm ready to get off for a while. We're all getting ready for dinner with the other band, Reckless Ambition. Those guys are huge. I love their sound. They're more metal than rock and they are fucking fantastic. No bias, but I do think our guys are better. Their sound is a mixture of different genres albeit, with a cool ass rock vibe. I don't know what I'm going to wear. I'm trying not to think about the Ivy chick.

She is so gorgeous—any man's wet dream. Hell, some women's too. I rumble through my suitcase trying find something adequate to wear. Lily comes in wearing a simple white strapless tube dress with purple stilettos. *Nice.*

"Having a bit of trouble?" she asks.

"That obvious, huh?" I joke. "I guess you can say that. My friend Brooke took me shopping before I left. Most of this is not what I would have picked for myself, so I'm at odds on what to choose."

"Here, let me have look," Lily offers. She pulls my suitcase to her before going through my things. "Girl, you have some awesome shit in here. I'm jealous. Your friend has awesome taste."

"I'll make sure to tell her that," I reply, but I'm not so sure. It reminds me I need to give her a ring. It's been two days. She's going to kill me for making her wait this long to find out how everything is working out so far. I admit that Brooke has great style, it's just not my style, so I'll have to do some adjusting.

"What about this beauty?" Lily pulls out an olive-colored bandage dress. "This is fucking sexy. You can pair it with these," she says pulling out a pair of black stilettos. I haven't broken them in yet, but it wouldn't matter. I don't think those shoes are meant to walk in for very long anyway. Thank God, it's only dinner and we'll be sitting for the most part.

"I guess so," I say taking the dress from her hands. "Thanks for helping me find something. I'd still be sitting here lost, and I know the guys are almost ready to go."

The nerves are starting to kick in now. It was one thing when it was just us. Now we're going to be traveling alongside the other band. I don't want our vibe to change. I try to remain positive and not worry too much. I change into the dress and work to hide my bra straps. There is no way I could get away with going braless so at least this dress has straps. The girls need all the support they can get. I pull the dress down a little more, willing it to stay put. I have never worn this out, so I pray there are no wardrobe malfunctions. Again, at least I'll be sitting.

It was easy to be bold with the gym shorts in front of Diesel. I admit I was being a tease. It was a brazen moment that wasn't planned. I just went with it. I don't want to make an ass out of myself. Shit never looks as good on me as it does on the mannequin.

"Stop fussing with your dress, girl. You look fabulous." Lily smacks my ass, and I'm stunned. "Sorry. Your ass just looks nice in that dress. I wish I had a little more to work with," she says as she looks back at her own ass.

"You're hilarious. And maybe you're not the goody two shoes I *may have* assumed you to be," I confess.

"Looks are deceiving," Lily warns. "Don't let this innocent face fool you." She grabs my hand to pull me out the door. I snag my clutch purse on the way out.

CHAPTER
Four

DIESEL

THE RESTAURANT HAS ARRANGED A PRIVATE ROOM FOR us away from the public. I'm at the opposite end of the table from Lourdes, and it's a freaking good thing. The dress she's wearing tonight accentuates every curve of her body that needs to be worshiped. It bugs the shit out of me that I can't stick to the original plan of not even giving her a second thought. I'm not supposed to be thinking of all the ways that I want to fuck her every time I lay eyes on her. I try to give my attention to my menu and figuring out what the hell I want to order, but each time I hear her voice across the room, I sneak little peeks at her. She is absolutely stunning.

The arrival of Reckless Ambition gets everyone's attention. Conversations stop to welcome them. Jack and Mitch are the drummer and lead guitarist for the group. Anderson and Miles are the lead singer and bass guitarist. The guys take seats around the table to get acquainted with us. Anderson joins me at the head of the table and we hit it off instantly. He's a real down to earth guy.

"You ready for this tour, man?" Anderson questions with a grin. The grit of his vocals are impressive so it's crazy to hear how different his speaking voice is.

"Hell yeah, man," I assure. "Where's your back up vocalist?" I ask casually in regards to Ivy.

"Oh, she stopped by the ladies' room first. You know women," he says, nudging me.

When she finally walks in, she fucking commands the attention of the entire room. She's wearing a Rolling Stones T-shirt that is knotted under her breasts with jeans that are ripped from thigh to ankle. No heels. Just Converse sneakers. Her look screams that she doesn't give a fuck, yet her body has my dick throbbing. *Finally*. Someone else has his attention. I know right away that I will have her under me, even before her eyes meet mine and she makes her way over to find a seat next to me. Sorry, Desiree. If Ivy gives me any indication at all that she is down, I'm going to fuck the shit out of her. I'm not a saint. I can't keep foregoing temptation. My dick needs attention and right now it wants Ivy.

"Well, hello. You must be the infamous Diesel I keep hearing about," she states as she takes a seat next to me.

"You're the infamous one," I correct. What the in the hell could she have possibly heard about me? "I'm just someone trying to get where you guys are." Anderson pats me on the shoulder and lets me know that he is going to introduce himself to the rest of our band. Nobody has really ordered food yet because we were waiting for them to show up. We've kept the bartender pretty busy though. I've barely put a dent in my second gin and tonic.

"Oh. It's nothing bad. Desiree told us about your band and let us listen to your sound." She leans closer and picks up my drink. She looks me directly in the eyes—daring me to object. She takes a small sip before taking a bigger one. "*Hmmm.* So good. Gin and tonic?"

"Uh, yeah," I say without breaking her gaze. I'm caught off guard by her forwardness. She's already giving me the green light. "So, what did you think?"

"Of what?" she challenges. She knows what I'm asking.

"Of our sound," I play along.

"We're touring together, aren't we?" She winks. "I think you guys complement us perfectly. A perfect blend of perfection."

"Agreed," I grin. That means a lot coming from a member of a band that is already so established. We don't even have recognition yet.

"Make no mistake about it, Diesel," she adds. "You're fucking hot as hell. This face and body are going help you guys climb the charts. But your vocals and your band's sound is what's going to make you guys rock stars. You have the total package." I don't know how to respond to that. I blame it on the lack of current blood flow to my brain, because it's all at the head of my dick.

"Glad you think so," I finally manage to get out.

She moves in closer. "Oh, I do. And when all those women are lining up—just hoping for the chance to get a taste of your cock, I'll enjoy knowing that I have you for the next four months." I grab my gin from her and take a huge ass gulp. That was bold as fuck. Is she really going to do all the work for me?

"What do you mean you have me for the next four months?"

"I think you know," she says squeezing my leg under the table. That escalated fast. She is going to have to spell that shit out for me. I'll let her think she is in control for a few more minutes before I yank that illusion from her.

"I don't like to assume anything, Ivy. You've been so forward up to this point. Don't play coy now." I take another swig of my drink. I get a glimpse of Lourdes at the end of the table and her facial expression is telling. She can't hear the conversation between Ivy and I, but I'm sure our body language says it all. Ivy is damn near in my lap and she isn't giving a shit who notices.

"That's one thing I don't do, *Diesel*," she insists. "I don't play games. I see something I want, I take it. I'm calling dibs on this." She tries to reach for my dick under the table, but I grab her wrist. I have no doubt that she is used to getting her way. She's gorgeous, has a banging body, and a bank account with several trailing zeros and comas. None of that shit matters to me, though. I arch an eyebrow at her. She has no idea.

"Only one problem with that logic, doll," I tsk. "This is my dick and I say who can have a taste. I say who and I sure as fuck say when," I inform her. I shake my head because she fucked any chance of having me tonight. Her assumptions have earned her a lesson that I'm oh so willing to teach. The waiters bring out the food and I realize that everyone has ordered except us. I waved the guy off the first time the he made rounds, but I thought he would be back. Oh well. I'd rather eat left over chicken breast from last night.

"You don't mean that, Diesel," Ivy retorts.

"It was nice meeting you, Ivy. I look forward to rocking this tour with you guys." I'll just have to show her how serious I am. I give her the same wink she gave me earlier and her mouth drops. *Perfect.* Let that sink in. I rise from my chair and round the table to meet Miles, Mitch, and Jack. We exchange a few words before I tell them all I'm heading back to the bus. Lourdes can't even look at me. She probably thinks Ivy is on the way out with me. I will give Ivy what she wants if she tones that alpha female shit down. My dominant nature is itching to make her submit. Thing is, she is so far from being a submissive, it's comical. That's the beauty of it. Ivy meet my alpha. Say hello to your match. You've never come across a man like me. I'm immune to your charms and wicked ass sex appeal. This alter ego of mine is the one that is in full control. I just need to make sure he stays present. I need to get him reacquainted with Lourdes too. Not to make her submit, but to move past my desire for her. My dominant side demands respect, rewards the worthy, and above all, avoids fucking becoming attached.

I see Ivy hasn't moved from her seat. She's smirking with her arms folded. *Checkmate.*

"Night, everyone. See you in the morning." I get the hell out of the restaurant and don't look back. The bus is parked across the street in a paid lot. It's plain black so nobody has any idea it's a tour bus or who's inside.

Having the bus so close, I could have easily brought Ivy over and made use of that bed back there. Her loss. I heat up what's left of the chicken from last night and throw together another salad. I need to prep my shit before things get too hectic. Desiree calls me just as I sit down to eat to let me know that we have a photo shoot in the morning before rehearsal. The shoot is for a possible single CD cover, as well as some promo to push the word we're touring with Reckless Ambition.

I finish the call and resume eating my food before it gets cold. I watch the door for a bit before heading to take a shower. I half expected Ivy to follow. Then again, she was rejected. She isn't going to make it easy for me now. She wants me to regret my decision and pursue her. Her smirk was so telling. I will make sure I have a few bitches visit my dressing room tomorrow night as an appetizer. I have the stamina to pleasure a plethora of pussy. If she thinks I'll cave and play her boy toy for the length of this tour, she'll be waiting.

I'm sure Desiree wouldn't approve. She issued a warning, but I know what the fuck our contract says. If I decide to give Ivy this dick and she gets salty after it's over, she can't back out of our legally binding business agreement. I'm not a follow the rules or do as you're told kind of guy. I know the reality and consequences of my actions. I do what the fuck I want. I don't consider fucking Ivy shitting where I sleep now because technically she is not sleeping on this bus. We'll see if she smartens up and realizes it's my game to play, therefore my rules to make.

Lourdes

It's time to go back to the bus. We all stayed and closed the restaurant down with food, laughter, and just getting to know each other. Well, all except Diesel and Ivy. Diesel left first and then Ivy left maybe twenty minutes after he did. I faked a smile the rest of the night. I knew this was coming. I knew Diesel was going to be getting plenty of ass. I just didn't expect it to be before his first concert and with his fellow tour member. I'm sure everyone else came up with same conclusion about what the two were up to, but they didn't pay it any mind.

"What are you so deep in thought about, girl?" Lily joins me as we walk across the street. The guys are still deep in conversation.

"Nothing really. Just missing my friend Brooke. I really do need to call her," I lie. "I'm shocked no paps or crazy fans were out tonight hounding these guys," I say to change the subject.

"I was actually wondering the same thing, so I asked Xander about it at dinner," she confesses. "He says that the restaurant has an exclusive guest list and a long as hell waiting list to get a table. In other words, people with lots of money eat here. People with an exorbitant amount of money are not going to go all fangirl over some rock stars."

"True," I nod.

"The paps have to stay a certain distance away because the restaurant has some sort of no trespassing ordinance and can actually sue them if they violate it—kind of like a members only club. Because of that, they get a lot of celebrities here. Celebrities know they'll get a hassle-free dining experience. It's the reason they picked this place for their first meet."

"Pretty clever. You'd think more businesses would do the same thing."

"Yeah, but it takes a lot of money, and probably rubbing of palms, to pull this type of privacy off." Lily chuckles.

"Isn't the saying greasing the palms?" We look at each other and fall into a fit of laughter. Lily is great. She isn't Brooke, but I'm thankful she's here with me. She helped get my mind off Diesel and what he's doing on that bus with Ivy.

We're standing outside our bus now, but the guys don't make an effort to carry this meet and greet onto the bus. We're only out here for about ten minutes before a white stretch limo pulls up. So I guess they were just waiting on their ride.

Oddly, Ivy doesn't come out to leave with them. I'm guessing she's staying the night on our bus. *Here we go.* I suck in a deep breath and board the bus with Lily and the guys. I wasn't supposed to feel whatever this is. My heart is racing. The reality of it all is overwhelming right now. I just need to get out of this ridiculous dress, shower, and go to sleep. I don't want to think about any of it. I don't want to feel this way. *He's. Not. Mine.* I excuse myself from the group by saying that I'm tired and going to call it a night. I use the shower at the front of the bus because there is no way in hell I'm going through that bedroom. My shower is the quickest one yet. I make it to my bunk in under twenty minutes. Thankfully exhaustion takes pity on me and pulls me under so my mind doesn't have time to linger on shit I shouldn't be thinking about—or worse yet, hear them fucking.

DIESEL

"Morning, dip shits," I say as I stroll through to the kitchen. Everyone is up and in our little living area, except Lourdes. Lily peers over her gossip magazine to give me the finger. I'm starting to like this girl more and more. She has a little sass to her. She came off as meek, at best, in the beginning. I guess she just had to get comfortable with us.

"We already had breakfast, your royal dip shit." She grins. "We saved some for you."

"Aye. Where is it?" I look around the stove, but don't see it. Why can't I smell what they cooked?

"It's in the cereal box above the refrigerator." She places her magazine over her face and laughs her ass off while Keyser and Xander join in.

"That's real cute," I say shaking my head. I can't help laughing along with them.

"She got you, man," Gable instigates.

"Yeah. I made omelets for your asses yesterday and today we're eating cereal." I pull fresh eggs out the fridge to scramble up some egg whites. I'll have that with some oatmeal. I'm not eating that sugary shit.

"Sorry, Diesel," Lily says. "Nobody felt like getting in the kitchen to do anything after staying up last night."

"Where's Lourdes?" I ask casually.

"Oh, she didn't stay up with us last night. She was the

first to hit the sack so I thought she would be the first one up," Xander says. "I guess we need to get dressed for our photoshoot that you failed to mention," he teases.

"Shit, man!" I forgot to tell them about that. I crashed before they returned from the restaurant.

"No worries, dude. Desiree called and bugged the shit out of us early this morning when she couldn't get a hold of you. Why do you think we're all up so early?" Keyser gives me a knowing look. I glance at the clock in the kitchen and see that it's a little after eight. These guys' idea of early is warped. "We didn't tell her about the ass you already tapped last night. She would have your balls. Where is she anyway?"

"What? She who?" What the hell is he talking about? I didn't get any ass last night. Then a light bulb goes off.

"Ivy, fucker. We didn't see her get off the bus when their limo came for them last night." Ivy must have left after I did last night and they all assumed she was meeting me. That means Lourdes thinks I smashed Ivy last night, too. Is this why she went to bed early or why she still isn't up yet? My damn reputation precedes me a little too well, but this time they're all wrong.

"I don't know where Ivy went last night, but she didn't come here. I didn't touch her."

"Wow. I just knew you had hit that. She was damn near in your lap trying to give you the pussy, man." The guys nod in agreement. They have no idea.

"Well, I didn't bite. I'm going to get ready for this shoot. I suggest you fuckers do the same," I say, bringing my meal with me.

CHAPTER
Five

Lourdes

FEEL A WARM HAND NUDGING ME TO WAKE UP AND NEARLY hit my head on the top bunk when I sit up startled. "Wake up, Lourdes. We'll be getting off the bus in roughly thirty minutes," Diesel informs me. When I see it's him, I snatch my arm away.

"Yeah, okay." I grab my phone from the charger next to me to look at the time and to avoid eye contact with him.

"Ivy wasn't here on the bus last night Lourdes. I didn't fuck her," Diesel says before walking away. My shoulders instantly relax with relief. Then I get pissed all over again because why do I even care? The fact that he just told me that means he knows that I do. *Ugh.* I need to find something to wear. That Ivy chick could wear a freaking paper bag and rock that shit. She didn't even try to get dressed up for the restaurant. She wore jeans, a T-shirt, and sneakers. She still had Diesel's attention from the moment she walked into the room. It was so apparent that she had set her sights on him too. They may not have fucked last night, but it is inevitable. Their sexual tension was so strong, it consumed the entire room.

The temperature is bearable today, considering we're smack dab in the middle of January. I still nearly froze my ass off trying to be cute last night. I'm used to the almost nonexistent winters of the south. My phone's weather app says it's fifty-five degrees out so a hoodie and jeans it is.

"Are you ready yet, Lourdes?" Lily calls from the other side of the door. I open the door to see that she's dressed in cute jeans, a sweater, and ankle boots. "Are you ready?" she asks again.

"Sure am," I answer. My University of Alabama hoodie and jeans is what I'm sticking with. I have nobody to be cute for. My give a fuck is broken.

"Oh, okay," she says unwilling to push. "Well, the guys are waiting for us outside in the black Yukon. Desiree sent someone to pick us up." I nod and we leave without another word. I'm in a funky mood this morning and I can't shake it. We get into the SUV and the guys are trying to strategize what their album cover should look like. I don't look any of them in the eye. I head straight back to the third row. I pull my earphones from my pocket and plug it into my phone. I need to drown out my thoughts. Rihanna's *Needed Me* is the first song to shuffle through. I close my eyes and attempt to get lost in the lyrics. I haven't been in a funk like this since my initial break up with Diesel. I hate feeling vulnerable—like I'm waiting for the remaining pieces of my heart to disintegrate. I hate giving anyone the power to completely destroy me.

The ride to the photographer's studio is a short one. Lily nudges me to let me know that we've arrived. I didn't even know she came to sit back here with me. I just assumed she would stay closer to the front with Xander.

"Are you feeling okay?" she whispers.

"Yeah. Just have some stuff on my mind is all. Nothing that's a concern," I say, plastering a fake smile on my face.

"Okay. You can always talk to me if you ever need to." She squeezes my hand before pulling me out with her. Now that the men are out of the car, I get a good look at them. They're all wearing black t-shirts with jeans. The look is so casual, yet so sexy. My eyes fall on Diesel and I have to look away. His shirt hugs him and I can make out his defined abs. Why does he have to be so damn hot? I give my attention to a pebble on the ground like it is the most interesting thing I've ever seen. I kick it around while I wait for them to head toward the studio. Another car pulls up. It's Desiree. She gets out wearing a red pant suit with matching heels. I guess I'm the only underdressed one but whatever. I'm not cold and I'm comfortable.

"Morning, boys. Lily. Lourdes," she half ass greets. "This way." She catches up to Diesel and the two of them talk on the way into the studio, but I can't hear what's being said. Whatever it is, Diesel doesn't seem to be too happy about it. I can see the wrinkle in his forehead from here. *Why is he frowning?*

The photographer, Antonio I think his name is, greets us once we're inside and then shows Lily and I where we can sit so that we're out of the way.

We still have prime seating though. Antonio's back is to us, but we can see the guys clearly as they take direction from him. They get into a grove instantly and all you hear is the camera.

"Okay. Diesel I need a few shots with just you." That wrinkle in his forehead is back. This must have been what he and Desiree were talking about.

"I don't see why that's necessary," he complains.

"I explained that you guys are going to be featured in *Rock Solid* magazine as new and upcoming artists. The band as a whole will be featured as well, but they want some solo shots of you. Don't bust my balls here, Diesel," Desiree pleads. "I had to pull some strings for this."

"It's okay, man," Xander assures. "You're our front man. They just want some shots of all your sexiness. We're not tripping. You got this, stud," he jokes, lightening the mood. The guys make smooching noises like they're blowing him a kiss to which he shoots them the middle finger.

"Okay, let's do this," he says to Antonio.

"That's what I'm talking about," Antonio says getting hyped. He throws him some shades. "I have an idea. Put those on and then lose the shirt and shoes."

"Just trust him, Diesel. He's the best at what he does," Desiree warns. Antonio pulls back the sliding glass door that leads to a patio overlooking Los Angeles. "Come," he instructs. He tells Diesel to stand against the railing and do whatever feels natural.

And holy hell does he give us a show. What is it about a man in jeans and bare feet? Diesel is the fucker who destroyed my heart. I'm not even supposed to be on this tour. Yet here I am, lust driven and completely turned the fuck on, as I watch him transition through poses for Antonio. He inches his jeans down just a tad, but enough to expose that vein that sits along his V, where my tongue wants to trace. Memories of his beautiful cock compete with my desire to remain angry with him and it pisses me off. I can't forget about his deceit. I can't forget why I promised myself I would never be with him that way again. Just last night, I thought he fucked Ivy for God's sake. Maybe I just need to get laid. I haven't been with anyone since him. I'm choosing to believe that he and Sevyn wouldn't be that dirty to let me sleep with the brother without my consent. That is the only reason I can move forward and give us a chance to be friends again. I will never forget though. It's going to take time for the anger that rears its head every time I remember the relationship he tarnished, to completely dissipate.

"That's a wrap, man. You killed it," Antonio says while playing back pictures through the viewfinder. Diesel just gives him a thumbs up. Desiree thanks the photographer for his time and informs the guys they have one hour to get something to eat before set up and rehearsal at the venue they're performing at tonight.

"Fuck yeah," Keyser hoots. "Almost show time on the big stage." This starts a conversation about the thousands of fans that will be in attendance. Some of their loyal fan base from Hundred Degree's bar is even making the trip down to see them play their first show. I trail behind them and pull out my phone to call Brooke. She's between classes so we keep the conversation short. I let her know we made to Cali.

"How are you getting along with Diesel?" She gets straight to the point.

"Decent," I say in code. "Better than expected." Brooke takes the hint that I can't go into specifics.

"Is he there with you now?"

"Yeah. We're all heading to get something to eat and then they have to get ready for tonight."

"Gah. I wish I could be there. I'm glad you finally called me though. I thought I was going to have to come find you. I'm happy to hear your holding up and you two didn't kill each other on sight," she jokes.

I'm not sure holding up is what I'd call how I'm feeling at the moment, but I don't elaborate. "You'd like Lily. She's sweet, but can hold her own." Lily is walking hand in hand with Xander, but she turns back to look at me when she hears her name. Apparently she was listening, so I'm glad I didn't say anything too revealing about Diesel and myself.

"I'm glad you have someone to hang out with since I can't be there. I bet Xander is happy that you two are getting along, as well." I hadn't even thought about that.

"The guys are okay. They like playing cards and dominos—real down to earth," I share.

"*Mhmm.* I have feeling that will change as soon as they find groupies to bang at every stop. They'll have some other games they'll like to play that won't include you ladies. Well, Lily will get to play with Xander, but that's going to leave you odd man out unless you find your own piece." I swear Brooke has no shame.

"Are you encouraging me to become a womanwhore?" I giggle.

"Your ass is forever making up words," she giggles with me. "Womanwhore? Geez, you're single. Find some unattached dick. It's easy for us. Men don't have a problem with no strings, one night stand fucking." I swear she's insufferable.

"You know I can't just sleep with some random guy," I whisper into the phone. "I'm not that...sexually free."

"And note that I didn't say crap about sleeping. Fuck 'em and leave 'em in the city you find them in. You definitely won't have time to worry about what Diesel is getting up to then," she adds. I guess I wasn't fooling her too much. She hit the nail on the head. She knows the underlying source of my worries. I won't admit it to her though.

"I'm not worried about that anyway. That's inevitable. I see it coming," I say in regards to knowing that Diesel is going to definitely fuck someone else. Ivy will be one of them. "Anyway. I know you have class. We'll talk later. I'll tell you all about the concert when I call you back."

"You better," she tells me. "Talk later. Find you some disposable dick, woman." She is like a dog with a bone and there is absolutely no reasoning with her.

"Bye, woman," I say before ending the call. Gus has food waiting for us back at the Yukon. Well, if you can call it that. I see Diesel frowning again until he see that he got a chicken sandwich. We eat on the way to the venue. There is no talking this time because everybody is busy stuffing their face before the SUV reaches its destination.

It is so cool to watch the guys warm up and listen to the way their music sounds in the bigger space. They start with a cover of Nickelback's *Never Again* and I feel myself getting excited for them. With each beat of the drum and pluck of the guitar strings, elation begins to take over. Diesel's gritty vocals croon into the mic and I can see the genuine appreciation from Reckless Ambition. When our guys perform, their talent can't be denied. My body begins to move of its own accord. You can feel the energy when they turn it up a notch. Diesel's grip on the mic flexes the muscles in his forearm and his tattoo sleeve is sexy as fuck. He rocks back and forth as he delivers the lyrics.

Ivy hops on stage with them and the guys don't miss a beat. She takes one of the mics and start singing an octave below Diesel.

I just knew he was going to be pissed that she was intruding on their music. Instead, a fucking smile crosses his lips while he sings to her. Their vocals are a perfect blend. She runs a hand through her short red pixie-cut hair as she gets into the lyrics. Diesel steps toward her and manages to grab a fist of the short strands before pulling her toward him in a move so dominant, you can see the shock on his guys' faces. They don't know that side of him and he's showing it to this bitch. I recognize his alter ego that just joined them on stage and I want to throw up. She just continues singing, but it's obvious that she likes the attention he is giving her. I can't look away. It's like a train wreck. I'm too sober for this shit.

"Our guys are fucking amazing," Lily squeals next to me—oblivious to the jealous daggers I'm throwing at Ivy.

"I know," is all I can say. I watch as the two continue to flirt. I envy Ivy's go for what you want attitude. She wants Diesel and she's making it known. She looks like the kind of woman to get what she wants, too. I can admit she's sexy. And pretty—still a bitch though. She can have any guy she wants. Why does she have to go after Diesel?

They wrap up the song and everyone applauds.

"You can't have my back up vocalist, Diesel, you pretty motherfucker you," Anderson yells up to the stage mockingly.

"That may not be a bad idea," Mitch chimes in.

"What?" Diesel asks confused.

"Have Ivy, or one of us, join in on one of the cover songs you perform. Not on your original tracks, but on a song we all know. This will add yet another layer to this tour for the fans to see us rocking out together," Mitch suggests.

"True," Diesel replies excitedly. "I think that would give us an even bigger edge with our quest for band recognition." Our guys nod in agreement.

"Done deal," Anderson assures. "Not tonight for your debut on the road. Maybe our next stop after we've had some time to plan which songs you all want us to come in on."

I guess it would make sense that our guys would be open to sharing their spotlight with Reckless Ambition. That's going to give them instant credibility and recognition. I'm happy for them.

"Done," Diesel echoes. "Can't wait to tell Desiree. She is going to flip her shit. She will love this idea."

"I love that manhandling you threw in there," Ivy adds.

"We can play off each other just like that during the show too. I think the women will eat that shit up. You will make all their panties wet."

"I do that anyway," Diesel winks.

"Cocky much?" Ivy challenges.

"Want to see?" Diesel retorts grabbing his dick. "I bet your panties are wet right now."

"Whoa, you two," Anderson says waving his hand. "That's TMI for the rest of us."

"Yeah, why don't the two of you fuck each other's brains out already," Mitch laughs. "We all see it coming. It's like a damn soap opera playing out slowly. Just do it already."

"Don't I get a say in this?" Ivy asks in mock disgust.

"Ivy, if you had your say, you would have fucked him last night. We know you and how you are when you want something. Hush, and let us play your wingmen so we can help you get on that," Mitch jokes.

"I have nothing," Ivy concludes. "You guys know me too well."

CHAPTER
Six

DIESEL

I T'S ALMOST SHOW TIME. I TAKE A MOMENT TO GET IN THE zone. Our dressing room is nearly double the size of what we're accustomed to and definitely more pimped out. I fix myself a glass of bourbon to still my nerves. I usually don't get nervous. In Alabama, we were the shit. The audience we're performing for tonight has never heard us before. Will they like our sound…our original songs? I finish my drink in three gulps. I look around the room and take it all in. Xander and Keyser are talking on the other side of the room. Gable is mindlessly flipping through channels on the TV. Desiree came in about thirty minutes ago to give us the *you-got-this* speech. Now it's fifteen minutes until we hit the stage. I pour myself two more shots of bourbon.

"You okay, man?" Xander asks, walking over after he sees me on my second drink.

"Yeah," I reply, taking a swig. There's a soft knock on the door before it opens. It's Ivy and the guys from Reckless Ambition coming to wish us luck.

"I still remember our first time performing in front of a huge audience. That was when reality hit that we were really on our way," Anderson recalls. Ivy surprises me by taking my hand.

"You guys are the real deal, Diesel. We knew the minute Desiree played your demo. We never would have agreed to tour with you guys otherwise. Those fans out there are going to love you," she reassures. She squeezes my hand and I feel a sense of calm come over me. This is what I needed.

It's hard to shake years of feeling like a failure. When the man you look up to drills it in your head that you'll never amount to anything, you start to believe it. I wish my sperm donor could see me now. I bring Ivy's hand up to my mouth and kiss it. Now I'm ready.

"Thanks, guys," I say while looking at Ivy. We hear our introduction to take the stage. The guys go ahead of me. The lights dim to make the stage completely dark with the exception of a few spotlights. My guys take their places and within seconds their intro music fills the room. Adrenaline runs through my veins as I begin to feel the music. We're opening with our rendition of I Prevail's *Blank Space*. The crowd goes fucking crazy the minute the first lyric leaves my mouth. From that point forward, I'm on. I settle into the performance I usually give. I flirt and tease the women in the front row. I see flashes from cameras going off like crazy. I can't see Lily or Lourdes, but I know they're somewhere close.

By the third song, my shirt is clinging to me—dripping with sweat—so, I take it off. The women go fucking insane. Yeah, I know just what I'm doing. I'm sure there is not one dry pussy left. I've already had tits flashed at me. We transition into our original music by the fourth song and holy shit do they eat it up.

My guys are on fire tonight. Song after song, the audience gets even more rowdy. Their appreciation for our music is humbling. Everything we've worked so hard on is paying off right now. We close out our performance with a song that is so significant to me. I sing Leave it All Behind, leaving it all on the stage. It was the song I wrote for Lourdes. It takes me back to a place where things were good with us. Now I desperately try to think of it as just another song. The lights fade and we make our exit. The crowd is still begging for more. I'd say we knocked it out of the park. It feels fucking amazing. When we get back to our dressing room, Ivy is waiting there.

"You guys fucking killed it," she praises. "I knew you would."

"Thanks," I tell her. Keyser, Xander, and Gable thank her as well.

"Can I see you for a minute?" She motions for me to follow so I do, for now. We stop at a door that has her name on it.

"Look at you all special with your own room," I tease.

"Yeah. We each get our own room. It's one of the things we stipulate that we get. We need time to get in the right mind space before a show and prefer to have our own rooms." She moves aside and let me walk in first.

"Well, it's definitely a nice set up," I comment, taking everything in. "But let's be honest. Did you really bring me to your dressing room to show me how nice it is, or did you bring me here to show me something else?" I'm feeling good right now. She's caught me in a euphoric mood. I can give her a taste of my dominance so that she'll see why that alpha female shit she tries with me would never work.

"Umm. Well, I did want to get you alone," she says walking slowly up to me. She tries to touch me but I move out of reach.

"I didn't say you could touch me Ivy." The smile she's wearing falters.

"Can I touch you?" She looks unsure.

Someone's finally catching on.

"Turn around," I command without answering her question. She turns without hesitation. That was the right response. I'm glad because now I get to unleash what I've been wanting to do since the moment she walked into that restaurant. I tilt her head to one side so that I can place soft kisses on her neck. "You want me to fuck you before you go on stage, Ivy?" She nods and lets her body melt into mine. This is going to have to be quick because she has maybe ten minutes before the intermission is over.

I bend her over toward her dressing mirror and place her hands on the counter. Her eyes close in anticipation. The bright lights from over the mirrors shine down on us, and I have an idea. "Open your eyes, sweetheart. Watch me give you the dick you've been craving." She obliges and pushes her ass back toward me. I give it a smack before I kneel slowly to peel her tight leather pants down to her ankles. She isn't wearing any panties. My dick hardens instantly at the sight of her bare pussy from behind. I inhale her essence and begin to throb with want. I grip the side of her thighs and take my time dragging my hands along them. When I'm back to standing, I pull her bare ass against my jean clad cock, letting her feel how hard I am.

Her hooded eyes can barely focus on me in the mirror. I grab her chin to get her to look closely. "You stop watching and I'll stop fucking," I warn. "Got it?"

"Yes," she answers breathily. "Just fuck me. Please, Diesel," she begs. I reach into my pocket for the condom I knew I would need when she brought me here. I make a show of undoing my jeans. That gets her attention. To her surprise, I'm commando, too. I stroke my dick a few times for her benefit because this motherfucker is already cocked, loaded, and ready to go. I sheath myself to the hilt. I slap her ass once more and she points it toward me. Her pussy opens to receive me and I slide right in. She clenches immediately and the sensation is fucking awesome. I give her a few short strokes first—giving her slow and easy. When she begins to rock her ass against me, I know she is ready for me to go deeper. I grab a fist full of her hair and that is the only warning she gets. I plunge balls deep, enjoying the tightness of her pussy milking me.

"Dieeeeeeeseeeellll," she screams. "Fuck me harder." Holy fuck she's loud. I should have known she was a screamer. I'm going to fuck the alpha right out of her ass. Oh yeah, she submitting now. Hearing her begging for my dick, spurs me on. I give her exactly what she's asking for. Driving into her over and over again.

"Is this what you wanted, Ivy?" I tease.

"Yesssssssss," she moans. I love that she can't form a fucking coherent reply to save her life. I reach down with one hand and play with her clit. Her legs begin to tremble, and she's struggling to continue to watch us. I can feel the familiar tingle in my balls, but I'll be damned if I come first. I give her clit a pinch and she fucking explodes on my dick. She gives up trying to watch altogether as her orgasm rolls through her. I pump into her a few more times before I some with her. We hear them announce her band from the stage, but she just stands there with my dick still inside her. "I need a minute," she says dazedly.

"You don't have a minute, doll," I gloat. I slide out of her but she still looks discombobulated. I grab a few tissues from the counter next to her and wipe her pussy and she nearly comes undone from the aftershocks. A heavy knock at her door is followed by a male's voice yelling that it's show time. She doesn't answer. She slowly pulls up her pants, and I can't keep from chuckling as I help her. I wipe my own dick off and tuck it back into my jeans.

"That was fuuuccking amazing," she finally gets out.

"Yeah. Now you have a show to do so you have to pull it together." I can hear music begin to play as we speak.

"That was some nut," she surmises. "Oh, we have to do that again."

"Maybe. Now get your sexy ass on stage." I grab her by the waist to help her out the door. The smile that forms on her lips tells me that she is enjoying my fuss over her a little too much. We're not even completely out into the hallway before running into Lily and Lourdes. I'll never forget the look on Lourdes's face when she sees my hands around Ivy's waist. She tries to appear unaffected, but I saw it. It was the look of heartbreak. I know that look because I've put that look on her face before. *Fuck!* I knew this was going to eventually happen, but I still hate seeing it.

"Your guys are on stage," Lily announces. Then it's like she gets a clue. "Oooh, you two have been screwing around. Diesel you're going to get her in trouble," Lily says shaking her finger at me. Ivy just smirks.

"I am the show so it's fine if they want to start without me." She grabs my dick in front of them. "There will definitely have to be a few more rounds of that, handsome." She twists her ass toward the stage because she knows I'm watching.

Lily is shaking her head but Lourdes has yet to say a word, until now.

"Come on. Let's see if we can get a good place to watch the show," she says while walking off. *Just damn.*

This sinking feeling in my chest is not supposed to be here and I fucking hate it. I go back into the dressing room they have set up for us. The guys are lounging on the sofa watching Reckless Ambition's concert on the big screen. They look up when I come in and the shit eating grin that Keyser lets loose tells me they already know.

"So. Ivy was late getting to the stage. Did you have any-thing to do with that?" Keyser gets straight to the point.

I wave him off, but's it's no use.

"Desiree is going to kick your ass," Xander says matter-of-fact. Whatever, Desiree doesn't manage this dick, so she just needs to stick to what she was hired to manage.

"How was it?" Gable asks. Now this surprises me. He normally doesn't get involved in our shit. He's more of the quiet, introverted one. We give him his space.

"Guys, we're not talking about this…c'mon. Stop giving me shit. Where are the hoes at? You guys need some groupie love or something." I shake my head and get up to finish off some more of the bourbon I had before going on stage. Truth is, my thoughts are on Lourdes, and her reaction to seeing me with Ivy, rather than the actual fucking. I didn't have any problems fucking bitches until she came back into the picture. What the hell is this feeling? Guilt?

"Fine. Be that way, man. And for your information, we're chilling on having groupies back here tonight. This is only our first show. We want to let it all soak in and enjoy the experience. There will be plenty of time for that. Trust me," Keyser explains.

"Damn, they're killing it," Xander says bringing everyone's attention back to Reckless Ambition's performance on the screen. I'm thankful for the reprieve.

The band is nearing the end of their set when Lily comes waltzing in to join us and she's alone.

"Where's Lourdes?" Xander and I ask simultaneously.

"Don't cock block, boys," she slurs. "She's just right outside the door with some sexy guy she met. He's hot as shit. I only have eyes for you though, Xander." She's giggling and it is so obvious that she's had one too many tonight. Xander grabs her and pulls her to him, before giving me his *han-*

dle-that look.

"On it," I say to him. I swing the door open and I see some fucking douche bag with his hands plastered on Lourdes's ass trying to bring her closer to him. And she's fucking letting him. *What the fuck?* Then she stumbles a little bit from him tugging on her. She's drunk. I swear I see red spots of rage.

"Get your fucking hands off of her before I break them, you stupid fuck!" He looks up at me briefly before retuning his attention back to Lourdes. He waves one hand to dismiss me.

"Leave us alone, Diesel," Lourdes slurs, sounding similar to Lily. Mad is not even the right adjective at the moment. This suicidal motherfucker squeezes her ass harder, and I lose it. The guys come out into the hall just as I yank his dumb ass away from Lourdes and pin him against the wall. I'm about to punch his fucking face in when she grabs my wrist.

"Don't, Diesel," she manages to get out. Only she can't hold on. She falls flat on her ass.

I shove blondie against the wall one more time before I reach down for Lourdes. My guys are at my side by this point. Gable must have told him to get the fuck away while he could. I want to hold her and yell at her all at the same time. I can't show my cards though. I can't let on what I'm really feeling. I help her up and she clings to me to stay upright. And this is what the fuck this dirt bag wanted? She can barely stand, let alone walk. My blood is boiling. If looks are anything to go by, Xander is pretty pissed too. We can hear Anderson and Ivy wishing everyone a goodnight so we know it's time to go. There will be no after party tonight.

"I'm going to help Lily to the bus. I'm so pissed at both

of them I could spit," he says. We don't really see him phased by much. He is irate right now and has every reason to be. I don't want to even think about if they hadn't made their way back to our dressing room. "You got my sister?"

"Yeah. Let's go. Their asses are going to hear about this tomorrow," I assure.

"Definitely," he agrees. He heads toward the back where our bus is parked and Keyser and Gable follow him. Lourdes needs to grab her clutch first so we go back inside our dressing room for her to grab it. When we come out, we run into Ivy and the guys.

"What do we have here?" Ivy is the first to speak up.

"You remember Xander's sister Lourdes? Well she had a just a little too much to drink."

"A little?" she smirks.

"Shut it, you whorish bitch. You may have fucked him tonight, but he's leaving with me so just suck on that, cunt!" I'm caught completely the fuck off guard. I've never heard her speak like this, let alone flat out verbally attack someone. The guys look on, stunned, with questions in their eyes of what the hell is going on. Ivy just laughs.

"Sounds like you're jealous, Lourdes. I'll let that jab slide because you're drunk, but just know that's the only pass you'll get." Lourdes stumbles again, but then gives her the middle finger.

"Lourdes, stop. Let's go. Sorry, Ivy." Lourdes is trying to push away from me, but if she thinks I'm letting her go she's crazy.

"Why don't you get rid of that hassle and join me on my bus? We're going to the same place. Or—"

"Not tonight Ivy," I say, cutting her off and hoping she understands. She pouts, but it's not happening.

"That's right skank. He cock blocks and I pussy block." Lourdes informs. "My pussy is better than yours…" she sings. Holy shit. I need to get her away from Ivy and fast before she gives everything away.

"I wouldn't know," I roll my eyes to assure Ivy. "Talk tomorrow. I have to get her back to the bus." Ivy leaves me standing there. Anderson fist bumps me when he passes.

"Good luck with that, man," he says before they continue on their way. Lourdes is dragging so I throw her sloppy, drunk ass over my shoulder. I pray she doesn't say shit on the bus to get us busted. I didn't see this shit coming.

CHAPTER
Seven

Lourdes

I CRINGE AT THE SUNLIGHT IN MY FACE. I TRY TO BLOCK IT with my hand but there is a body snuggled in behind me and I can barely move. It takes me a few moments to realize I'm in the bedroom on the bus and that body is Diesel. *What in the ever loving fuck?* His arm is wrapped protectively around my waist. For a second, I let myself enjoy the feel of him. But then memories of last night crash these feelings of bliss. He fucked Ivy. I try to pull away from him, but my head protests the sudden movement.

"Ahhhh," I cry out. My freaking head is pounding like I've been hit by a two by four. This wakes Diesel. The gorgeous fucker lazily wipes the sleep from his eyes. Why does he have to be so beautiful? I can't even look at him. I shouldn't be jealous, but I am. I try again, albeit a bit more slowly, to get up.

"Are you okay?" He looks concerned. My head feels like shit, I have cotton mouth, my stomach feels queasy, and my body hurts. I tell him none of that.

"I'm fine," I lie, trying to get away. He pulls me back down next to him and my stomach rolls. I grab my head in desperation to stop the throbbing.

"Fine, huh? Lay down Lourdes. Let me take care of you, baby." We both go quiet. He's the one to spring from the bed this time. I think he realizes his slip up.

"Just lay here, okay?" He's still wearing his clothes from last night. "I'll be right back." I answer him by pulling the covers back over me. I couldn't get very far even if I wanted to. He leaves the room and I'm left alone to replay what happened last night. I don't ever want to drink that much again. What the hell was I thinking? Then I remember the hurt I felt seeing Diesel and Ivy coming out of her dressing room. She was even late for her own performance. I needed to drown those fucking feelings in alcohol. I went straight to the bar to order myself a drink. I don't even recall how many shots I had. I just wanted to feel numb. Lily didn't even ask why. She took almost as many as I did.

From that point on, things are kind of fuzzy but I do remember flirting my ass off with some cute blond guy. I'm sure I made an ass out of myself. God, I don't even want to know. I need to pee. I will just have to move slowly. I pull the covers back. I'm wearing just a t-shirt and panties—no bra. Did Diesel undress me too? *Ugh.* I'm literally on my hands and knees right now trying ease out of bed. Diesel would pick this moment to walk in. He's carrying a glass of water.

"Your ass in the air like that," he says giving me the okay sign with his other hand. He is lucky I'm sick as shit. He helps me get out of bed before handing me three pills with the water. "Here, take this. It's ibuprofen for that headache of yours. I'm sure your body is sore too, since you fell on your ass last night."

I turn away from him and take the pills. I'm so damn embarrassed. "Thank you," I whisper. "I just need to go pee." He turns me back to face him and lifts my chin.

"I'll help you," he offers. Like hell he will. "I won't look, even though you don't have anything I haven't seen before. Who do you think held your hair last night after you puked all over yourself? Who cleaned you up and changed you into something to sleep in?" I'm even more embarrassed now.

"Ugh," I moan. "Sorry you had to do all of that."

"I'm pissed that you put yourself in danger with that asshat last night, but never apologize for me taking care of you." The details of last night are muddy. I only remember bits and pieces, but suddenly I have a flash back of calling Ivy a cunt. "What's the matter?" he asks when I groan for the millionth time.

"Did I really call Ivy a cunt last night?"

"Among other things," he informs. "You were in rare form last night princess. It would appear that you can't contain your jealousy when you're intoxicated. You blew our cover to fucking pieces. Thank fuck the guys weren't around to hear your little rant." He smirks and the sexiness of it sends a tingle straight to my core.

"I don't want to hear anymore. I'm going pee before I embarrass myself even further."

"Oh, I'm sure you haven't heard the last of it. Wait until Xander gets a hold of you. He already laid into Lily this morning. He was fucking pissed. He doesn't know I stayed in here with you last night or I would be in the line of his wrath too," Diesel warns. "You're safe for now. Everyone got off the bus to go get breakfast."

"So why didn't you?" I ask as I head to the bathroom. There is no answer. I close the door behind me and finally empty my bladder. I don't even care if he can hear me. I'm past caring at this point. What can be worse than him witnessing me vomit on myself. *Gross.* I finish my business and start the shower. Need to wash my hair, and maybe the hot water will soothe my aching body. I realize I didn't bring any clean clothes with me after I'm already in the glass shower. Oh well. I'll wrap myself in a towel when I'm done.

The stream of hot water flowing down my body is exactly what I needed. It soothes my pounding head. I close my eyes and let the water run through my hair. I don't know how much time passes before I feel his presence. He opens the shower door and I'm frozen in place. Diesel grabs me by the hips and I feel powerless. I know I should kick him out, but right now, I just want to feel him. I need to feel him. *Fuck.* He fucked Ivy. *He fucked Ivy.* I repeat this over and over to myself, but I'm getting wetter by the second.

"Look at me, Lourdes." The warmth of his breath is mere inches from my lips, but I'm scared to open my eyes. I stubbornly leave them shut. "Have it your way, baby." It's the last thing I hear before his lips are on mine. I hate myself for giving into him so easily. My tongue swirl with his as I let him in.

"Mmmmm," I moan into his mouth. Headache completely forgotten. He lifts one of my legs and the hardness of his cock caresses my folds. It's been too long. I rub my pussy against him, desperate to dull the ache there.

"Tell me what you want, Lourdes," he says before resuming his assault on my mouth.

"You fucked Ivy," I say shamefully, resting my head on his shoulder.

"But I want you right now," he assures, evading my statement. "We can't go back to the way we were, but I can make your pussy cream. Let me make you feel good." He nudges his dick at my entrance, but it feels like he has doused me with cold water—a slap to the face with reality. I push him away.

"I can't do this. You're right. We can't go back to the way things were, but I can't be just your fuck either. I'm sure Ivy is up for the role, though." I will not cry. What the hell was I thinking? I'm so fucking weak. I get out of the shower and grab a towel. I need to put some distance between us. I watch as he runs his hand through his hair in frustration, but doesn't leave the shower.

I go into the bedroom and find some jeans, a shirt, and a hoodie. I'm dressed and off the bus in record time. I need some time on my own. I'll find somewhere within walking distance to eat.

DIESEL

I fucking caved and now she's running *again*. I had the will of a saint last night while I took care that she was cleaned up and changed. Her vulnerability in my hands unraveled something in me. It took me to a place I promised I would never revisit. I just wanted to hold her in my arms and know that she was safe. I didn't even care if Xander got up in the middle of the night and found me snuggled with her. His priority was Lily and Lourdes was mine. She will never know the level of guilt that wracked through me with each beat of her heart against my hand. I was sorry that I fucked Ivy. I was sorry that she saw us together and that it hurt her.

There's no denying that she holds my fucking heart in the palm of her petite fingers. She isn't aware of the power that she has. I don't want to be this man. I don't want to be weak for anyone. I have to let her go. I need to rebel against what she represents—my weakness. First I need to find her. I know my admission that we can't be more cut her deeply. If only she knew just how much I was ripping my own fucking heart out in the process. It's just the way it has to be. The one person who was supposed to love me unconditionally, broke me. I wasn't good enough so he threw me away. Lourdes was the first person since high school that I allowed to see me— the first person I put my heart at risk for and she stomped on it when she left that day. I had to pick up the shattered pieces without a chance to explain.

There is no amount of love that will make me relive that feeling of unworthiness. I fuck. I move on. Period. I throw on some clothes from my bag and leave out the door. She left on foot so she couldn't have gotten too far. I search for at least half an hour before I find her in a small mom and pop diner. She is sitting toward the back with her head down. A plate of uneaten pancakes and sausage is next to her.

I slide into the booth directly across from her. "Lourdes," I say gently but she doesn't lift her head. "Look at me, please." Still nothing. I reach my hand under her folded arms until I find her chin. When I lift her head, I'm fucking rocked yet again. Tears stream down her face. Her eyes are red and swollen. I did this and I can't fix it. I'm out of my seat and next to her within seconds. I just need to hold her. She needs to know how hard this is for me too. I will give her comfort. I just can't give her me. Not anymore. She cries in my arms and I'm defenseless. We get the nosy stares, but they can all just fuck off. We will sit here as long as she needs. She finally pushes away from me and wipes her eyes.

"I'm sorry, Diesel. That won't happen again." She wipes her eyes with the back of her hands before throwing a twenty on the table. "I'm ready to go now."

"Lourdes—"

"Don't. Please. I needed a moment and now I'm done. Let's not talk about it. Okay?" she says, cutting me off.

"Okay," I agree reluctantly. I can't give her what she wants so I respect her need to let this be forgotten.

We walk the ten minutes back to the bus in silence. I need to work on some lyrics or something. I need a distraction. This whole situation is a fucked-up mess.

When we get back on the bus, Lily and the guys are already lounging around. We're supposed to be pulling off in the next hour to head toward our next tour stop. We would have left last night, but the other band needed to get some things done here in Los Angeles before we left. Their bus will be following behind ours for the remainder of the time. Xander seizes the moment Lourdes gets on the bus to let her have it. He's yelling how irresponsible she was last night and that he didn't invite her on this tour to play babysitter. The jackass is so full of his own anger that he hasn't noticed the fragile state she is already in. A few sniffles come from her and he goes quiet. She then starts sobbing uncontrollably, just standing in the middle of the room.

"Oh my God, Lourdes. I'm sorry. You know I didn't mean it like that," he apologizes. I put my hand up then I put my arm around her and lead her to the bedroom. I'm so mad at his unobservant ass that I don't give a shit what he thinks about me comforting her. I bring her into the room and put the lock on the door.

"I'll be okay," she tries.

"I know. I'm not going anywhere so it's just me and you." I crawl into bed and pull her in with me. We'll figure this shit out later, but for right now we have each other. This room is our bubble. We don't have to deal with the reality in here. In here, it's just us.

"Okay," she agrees. She snuggles against me—her back to my front and we give each other comfort. It's not long before sleep finds us both.

Lourdes

I don't know how much time passes. I wake up in Diesel's embrace and the bus is now moving. I'm ashamed to say I had a relapse today. I wanted Diesel to take me in that shower, but his words crushed me. He was okay with just fucking me—just like he fucked her. That's all I've come to mean to him. No matter how much I tell myself that I'm done with him and that I don't care what he does, I know that I'm just lying to myself. He's still passed out, but I'm content to lay here. I'm not ready for us to leave our bubble. He mumbled about this room being our bubble as he drifted off to sleep. If this is all I can have with him, maybe that is okay.

I feel myself dozing back off to sleep, when there is a steady knock at the door.

"Why is this door locked?" I hear Xander question from the other side. "Diesel, open the door, man. Ivy's here for you." The bus must have stopped at some point during our nap. I cringe at the thought of her being here to see him. She's bringing reality to our fucking door—literally! Diesel sits up startled at the intrusion.

"Ivy is out there for you," I whisper. I'm afraid that any more words than that will get stuck in my throat. I attempt to get out of the way so that he can go to her, but he pulls me back down and kisses my forehead.

"Stay here," he insists. I'm not going to hide in here if that's what he's thinking.

Before I can object, he puts a finger to my lips to shush me. "Please. Okay?"

He gets up and opens the door and I can see Ivy and Xander standing on the other side. He walks out and closes the door behind him. I hadn't agreed to stay put, but when I hear arguing coming from outside the door, I decide not to move. Diesel is arguing with Xander. "I'm not fucking her, man," I hear Diesel growl. He tells him that I'm not feeling well and that I already feel bad enough about last night so there's no need to keep chastising me like a child.

"Don't get any ideas about my sister. Sorry, Ivy. But you fucked this girl last night and then you're locked in a room with my sister today?" Xander's tone has come down an octave, but is still stern. "Excuse me if I come off a bit protective, but wouldn't you."

"Look. I care about Lourdes. She needs someone too. When shit went down last night, you were quick to grab Lily, but you left your sister hanging. I was the one there for her when she needed someone. And I'm the one here for her today when she needs a friend. I don't see any one else taking on that role at the moment. You?" There is complete fucking silence. I have no idea what's happening now. "Okay. Then don't give me any hypocritical bullshit. If there's nothing else, I'm going back in the room. Ivy, we'll talk later. Please, in the future, call first." I can faintly make out Ivy responding, but I can't make out what she's saying.

Diesel comes back into the room and locks the door.

"Everything okay?" I don't want to come between him and my brother.

"It'll be fine. Let's see what we can find to watch on this damn TV," he says grabbing the remote. "I'll cook us up something to eat in a little bit, unless you're hungry now. You didn't eat your pancakes at the diner."

"No. I'm good for now. I did eat the eggs and fruit before you came in. My stomach is still a little queasy from the alcohol so I'm not ready for anything heavy," I assure.

"Cool." He flips through the channels until he finds my favorite show, *Elementary*. He then pulls me to him like before, only this time, we're not going to sleep. We're…cuddling. This is probably a terrible idea. As a matter of fact, I'm sure of it. For now I'm going to enjoy it, though. He chose me over Ivy this time. He chose our bubble.

CHAPTER
Eight

DIESEL

OURDES WATCHES ONE OF HER FAVORITE SHOWS, *Elementary*. She was a little more than excited to see that it was airing the new season. I think my brother watches this too. I've seen it recorded on our DVR back at the lake house. She is asleep now, snuggled underneath me. I flip through the channels as I feel myself getting drowsy. I need to get up and cook us something. I need to make her eat. To my surprise the door swings open and it catches me off guard. I thought I fucking locked that door. It's Xander, but I don't bother to move. The scene before him is what it is. He walks in and pauses when he sees his sister in my arms.

"You care about her don't you?" he starts.

"Of course I do, Xander." He has no idea the extent of it.

"Look, I apologize for my earlier accusations. Truth is, I wasn't there and you were. I'm honestly just glad she had someone when she needed it the most," Xander reassures me.

"Where's Ivy?" I know the bus hasn't stopped again since our last conversation.

"She's watching Keyser and Gable battle each other in dominos," he informs me.

"Any other members from Reckless Ambition here?"

He shakes his head. "Just her." I know I need to talk with Ivy. I'm not sure if there will be a round two. This is why I wanted to abandon the three fuck rule on the road. I don't want to give her false hope.

"I understand. If it were my sister, I would be just as protective." I ease my arm out from under her and leave the room. As soon as I enter the living area, Ivy is on her feet.

"Finally," she huffs. "What the hell?"

"Don't," I caution her. "Lourdes is my friend. I'm not trying to be a douche, but why are you here?" I'm not going to curb my concern to pacify her. Yeah, we fucked, but it was a mutual want. I'm not her boyfriend and I don't owe her any explanations.

"I wanted to see you. I don't make it a habit of just fucking someone and then not speaking with him." There is an uncomfortable pause in the room. The guys don't know how to react.

"Just stop, Ivy." I wanted her to come out and acknowledge that she wanted to see me, although it was uninvited, but she is making me regret giving a shit. On cue the bedroom door creaks open. Lourdes peeks out so I go to her.

"What do you want to eat?" She needs to eat something. "We have tuna salad already made." I don't know what else is in there, or what everybody else ate tonight, but I remember we have the tuna salad I made earlier.

"That sounds nice," she says softly.

"Well, go find something else for us to watch, and I'll bring some to you." She nods and closes the door again.

"Fuck you, Diesel. You fuck me, yet you pamper her. I'm getting off of this fucking bus right now. Consider my legs officially closed to you." She marches toward the front of the bus, I'm guessing to request that they let her off.

"Do you and Lourdes have a thing, Diesel?" Lily asks timidly. I know my actions toward Lourdes are confusing. Hell, it doesn't make sense to me either.

"I'm just being there for a friend, Lil," I assure. "We're just friends."

"Okay," she replies sounding unconvinced. I make some toast, pour orange juice, and plate some tuna salad before bringing our spread to the room. Lourdes has another episode of Elementary on pause.

"Is this show okay?"

"Yeah. We can watch anything you want." I'm fucking up and I know it. There is no doubt we both see this room as the place to indulge in what we're feeling. In this room we don't have to think about the reality of our actions. I set the tray down with the spread I created and she smiles from ear to ear. I climb into bed and pull her between my legs.

"What are we doing, Diesel?" she asks while putting the tray in her lap.

"Ignoring the world out there," I say, pointing toward the

door.

"I kind of like that idea," she says spreading tuna on toast. She passes it to me. I take a bite, but then I feed her the second bite. Yeah, were slipping further and further into dangerous territory. I repeat over and over to myself that I can't give her all of me. On the other hand, if this is all we can have, I'll gladly take it. We eat all the food I prepared and vegetate through at least three, hour-long episodes of her show, before she dozes off again. I power off the TV and snuggle in close until I fall asleep with her.

Tonight we will perform our second show. I'm in the living area writing music. Lourdes is in her bunk working on her account of our journey thus far. We both realized that we couldn't hide in our bubble forever. We were beginning to cast suspicion on ourselves, not that I give a shit at all.

Ivy is giving me the cold shoulder and I'm okay with that. I didn't know how to proceed with that anyway. It just all seemed wrong after the fact. The lyrics flow seamlessly and I can't get them on paper faster enough. Shit that I've previously internalized, comes full circle. I leave every last ounce of my troubling thoughts in the bars of the music. I'm in a zone when my phone goes off. I would ignore it, but it's Issues' *Blue Wall* playing. That's Sevyn's ringtone. Our relationship has been strained, for obvious reasons, so we haven't spoken much since he told me our father was dying. Maybe that is why he's calling.

"Yeah," I say when I answer.

"Hello, brother," he says hesitantly. "Do you have a minute?"

"What's up?" I just want him to get to the point. "Is our father dead or not?"

"Not yet. I'm calling because he is going away to London next week. He says it's just for one last visit while his health will allow, but I'm not buying it. Morgan Investments is located there. I think he may be trying to partner with them before making the announcement about his health to the shareholders and board members in a couple weeks." That's not good. If he brings someone else in, that can weaken Sevyn's controlling votes. We need him to have the majority vote. Another member can side with the shareholders, giving them the overall majority. That would ruin everything.

"Shit. How do we block that?"

"I have an idea, but you may not like it. I need to see you." I can hear the desperation in his voice. I need him to keep it together. We've worked too hard on this to let it fall apart now.

"Look. We're on the way to Santa Clara. Can you get a flight and meet us there?" The guys know I have a twin now so he can join us while we work through this mess. We need a solid plan. I'll hear out his idea, but we need to be in agreement. This affects us both.

"I can do that. I can get a flight out this evening actually," he agrees.

"Okay. We're playing at Levi's Stadium tonight, but I'll give your info to our driver. It will either be Gus or Stewart. They can make sure you have a ride from the airport. Wish you could come see us perform." We can't afford for him to accidentally be seen at the concert. Not before we pull off our plan.

"Me too. Soon, brother." I give him the info he needs before hanging up. I need to tell Lourdes so she isn't blindsided for a second time. She is typing away on her Mac on her bunk when I find her.

"Hey," she says looking up at me. She gives me a little smile.

"Sevyn is coming here," I rush out. I watch the smile disappear. We haven't even discussed the reason he was at the lake house. We just kind of buried it and now we're reopening those wounds.

"Why?" she questions. "I mean whatever. I don't care." She closes her computer and rummages frantically through the bag next to her. I reach over and still her trembling hands.

"Lourdes, I'm sorry. I'm sorry I haven't talked to you about my brother, but I will. I never wanted to hurt you. When Sevyn gets here, we'll sit down and discuss the reason we're carbon copies of one another. The reason he can't be seen with me. I didn't want you to be blindsided again so I wanted to be the first to tell you he's coming here."

"Okay." I let her hands go and she pulls earphones out of her bag. I need to give her some space. She won't even look at me now. She connects the earphones to her phone and cranks up the volume. I can hear Mochica's *Scared* coming from the tiny speakers. She turns to lie on her back and closes her eyes. I guess that's my indication that this conversation is over. Sevyn and I haven't shared our full story with anyone, not even my guys. Tonight I will tell Lourdes. She deserves that much. It's the most sincere apology that I can give. My redemption.

Lourdes

Sex in Numbers gave another fucking epic performance to-night. I'm so proud of them and so excited that I get to wit-ness their journey firsthand. We're heading back to the bus now and I'm nervous because I know Sevyn should be there by now. I bonded with him too, before I knew who he was. I know of one day that it was him and not Diesel and that's the day before the big blow up. I do appreciate Diesel's effort to make this right. I just don't know what the fuck I'm supposed to feel.

The guys enter the bus first, and I immediately hear the boisterous greetings between them. Lily and I are close on their heels. She does a double take when she sees the two brothers side by side. Xander filled her in that Diesel had a twin who was joining us on the bus for a few days, but that is the most any of them know.

My heart drops at the sight of them. The flashback of the last time I saw them together is too real. I can tell which is Diesel because he's wearing his Sex in Numbers rock tee. Other than that, it's fucking crazy how identical they are. Same haircut. Same tattoos. Same hot as fuck body. Same ev-erything.

"Okay. This is a little cray," Lily says interrupting their

hoorah.

"Diesel, I've never seen twins this identical. I only know who is who from your clothes. That is so damn freaky." The uneasiness between the two brothers is palpable. The question is why?

"Yet, we couldn't be more different," Sevyn promises with a half-smile.

"Yeah. He's the sensitive one," Diesel agrees.

"And he got all the jackass genes," Sevyn retorts.

"Hey, don't be mad because I'm hotter." Diesel gives him shit, but the banter between the two is harmless.

"Keep telling yourself that bro," Sevyn says, lightly shoving his brother. "Anyway, I hope you all are hungry. I killed the time by cooking a little something." It was then I smelled something heavenly. How in the hell did I miss the mouthwatering aroma coming from the kitchen?

"Something does smell pretty fucking amazing. What is it?" Keyser asks already on the way to the kitchen to investigate.

"I made my famous bistro burgers." Sevyn beams and Diesel groans.

"What's that?" Lily asks with widened eyes.

"The devil," Diesel answers for him. "He knows that fucking burger is my weakness. It's my goddamn favorite."

"Miss you too, brother," Sevyn says, blowing him a kiss. The similarity of their voices is kind of weird but I can note subtle differences now that I had a chance to hear more than just a few words from him. We're all in the kitchen now and I can see what Diesel is talking about. These burgers look absolutely sinful.

"What's in them?" Gable asks grabbing one to put on a plate.

"It's a bison beer burger with fried egg, bacon, and avocado on a poppy seed bun," Sevyn shares.

"Crack," Diesel says around a mouth full of burger.

"I thought it was the devil," Xander says grabbing a burger from and Lily.

"Okay. Devil crack," Diesel corrects while taking another big ass bite. They all laugh at him.

"This is so good, man. You're our guest and you're cooking? Can't say I'm sorry though. Where did you get the ingredients to make this? We didn't have this stuff here," Xander quips.

"Hell no. That's because Diesel tries to make us eat that healthy shit he eats," Keyser swears. Diesel just nods and continues to demolish his burger. I hurry and grab one after I see some of the guys are already going back for seconds.

"Yup. That's my brother. He's always been that way too. He can't resist my burgers though, as you can see," Sevyn admits. Diesel flips him off and goes in for another burger. "No. Your driver, Gus, was happy to stop by the store after picking me up from the airport. I knew these were Diesel's favorite and I wanted to surprise him. I also knew he would be cursing me for sabotaging the diet he's always on."

"You two do have the same level of fitness, though," Lily points out. She's being politically correct for Xander's sake. Fuck a level of fitness. They're both ripped and sexy as hell. Not too big and definitely not small. They have the right amount of mass and thickness. I always said I would have never pictured Diesel as a rock star. He looks more like a model. I have to look away before I'm caught drooling.

"Don't let him fool you," Diesel speaks up. "Staying in shape comes more naturally to him. He eats healthy too, but his body is more forgiving when he doesn't. I have to be more careful since I can't get to a gym regularly on this tour. I have to settle for the weights I have in the bedroom." They start to talk about work out regimens and I take my burger to the living area. To my surprise, Lily follows me.

"That Sevyn guy is kind of hot, right?" she asks looking over her shoulder.

"He's okay," I say nonchalantly. I'm not stupid. She's been trying to piece together what's going on between Diesel and me. Admitting that Sevyn is hot is the same as admitting what I think about his twin.

"Girl, you are blind as shit. I have a man, but I still have eyes." She fans herself, and I laugh. I look over at the guys—the twins specifically—and Diesel is staring at me. I don't know how we're supposed to have this talk that he promised.

We stay up until almost two in the morning before I call it a night. That only leaves Keyser, Diesel, and Sevyn still up. A quick shower and fifteen minutes later, I'm crawling into my bunk. Tonight wasn't so bad. I didn't know how'd I feel seeing Sevyn again. Funny how time has a way of healing things. Perspective changes and considerations can be given when you're not in a murderous haze of anger. This is the closure I needed. They haven't even sat down with me yet to explain what the hell was going on back then, but I know now that, whatever it was, it wasn't out of malice. Because of that, I'm really ready to put it all behind me.

I decide to text Brooke before I go to sleep. I haven't

been in touch with her as much as I intended, but then again, neither has she. It's a testament to how I'm *holding up* better than either of us could have anticipated. I let her know that I'm doing fine and that Diesel and I are on the mend. I also share that Sevyn just joined us and how much I wish she was here. I know she won't see this text until morning, but I couldn't go to bed without letting her know that I was okay. I set my alarm for seven so, hopefully, I can get up and get some writing done before everyone wakes up and starts moving around. I write best when it's quiet. I need to keep an everyday account of the band's journey. So far they've been on their best behavior.

CHAPTER
Nine

Lourdes

'M UP A FEW MINUTES BEFORE MY ALARM GOES OFF. I
stretch and take in the scrumptious smell wafting in the air.
I smell bacon, but I can't make out what else. My stomach
growls. Okay maybe I can eat before I write. If not, I'll just be
distracted by the enticing aromas coming from the kitchen. I
slide from my bunk and follow the scent. Holy hell, I wasn't
ready. Diesel is facing the stove, but he's wearing just pajama
bottoms. The muscles in his back are just so damn lickable.
It's like deja vu. I've lived this scene before, just a short time
ago. His bottoms sit low on his hips and I can't help but drool. I
know what's hidden by those pajamas. A tingle between my
legs has me looking away. I'm about to go back to my bunk

when he turns and catches me standing there.

"Morning, Lourdes," he says, smirking. I'm pretty sure I'm bright red. I try not to stare at his abs, but I fail. Then something catches my attention. There's no fucking tattoo on his left side. Diesel has the serenity prayer on his left ribs. Holy shit. It's Sevyn. His fucking smirk gets bigger when he sees that I realize my mistake. "Hmmm. You would be correct sweetheart," he says answering my thoughts.

"Morning Sevyn," I say, trying to appear unaffected. Lily is right. He is hot as shit. Then another realization hits. I didn't fuck him. Even though, I guessed as much, this confirms it. I never slept with Sevyn. I would have known something was up if Diesel's damn side piece just suddenly disappeared. The thought is comforting.

"Are you hungry?" He walks over to me and I can't move. I have butterflies in my vagina. This shit is so unfair.

"*Mhmm*," I manage to get out. He places a hand at the base of my back and I get goose bumps.

"Come. Let me make you something to eat." He winks. Is he really flirting with me right now? These Beck boys are a hazard to my libido. I feel like such a filthy whore for being so turned on right now. How can I be this attracted to both brothers? Damn them for being replicas and confusing my hormones. Sevyn guides me over to the counter where he has food spread out, but his hand doesn't leave my back. I can feel heat radiating there. I'm so consumed with his closeness, I don't see Diesel until he's standing next to us. He looks down at his brother's hand but he doesn't acknowledge it. Instead he tells us good morning and then rubs my ass when he passes to grab a plate from the cabinet. I should be pissed. They're toying with me. So why is my pussy on fire right now?

"I think those are my favorite shorts," Diesel says. They're the short gym shorts from my first night here on the bus. The ones he forbid me from wearing into the store. "What do you think about them, Sevyn?" I'm going to melt right here. Just a damn pool of hormones evaporating onto the floor.

Sevyn doesn't even try to hide that he is looking at my ass. "Well, she does fill them out nicely," he agrees.

"You guys need to stop," I say with an eye roll. Hopefully, they can't see what their little game is doing to me.

I turn to put a pancake on my plate with a couple pieces of bacon. Sevyn offered to make my plate, but I got it. I feel arms come up on both sides of my waist and latch on to the counter in front of me. I'm trapped between Diesel and the counter. I don't have to see the tattoo to know it's him. He's the brazen one.

"You like my brother's hand near your ass, Lourdes," he whispers. I can feel the hardness of his dick pressed against my ass. My pussy is throbbing now. I push against him a little. I need to stop this, but not before I get a little feel first.

"Shut up, Diesel," I all but moan. He grabs my ass with one hand and I let him.

"He can't have this. It will be my dick sliding into this wet pussy of yours before that happens," he tells me. "We may look alike, but it's my cock that you're horny for right now. Say the word and I'll take you right here. I don't give a fuck. I'd even let him watch." He turns to look over at his brother who is witnessing everything going on right now. Why does the thought of letting Sevyn watch sound so fucking hot all of a sudden?

"I'm not horny—" I start to lie. My words are cut off by the slip of Diesel's finger under my shorts and right into my wetness. His fingers glide through with a few swipes before he removes his hand. I can't believe that just happened.

"You were saying, Lourdes?" Sevyn says as Diesel licks my essence from his fingers. I push away from him and head for the table. Yeah, I'm busted. I liked that just a little too much. I should have been mortified that Sevyn just witnessed all of that, but I'm not. They join me at the table with smiles on their faces. These fuckers are something else. It's crazy that just two months ago I was so pissed that they tricked me. Now they sit here toying with me and playing their twin games and I'm turned on.

"You guys are something else," I accuse. "Anyway. You said you wanted to talk, Diesel, so talk before everyone else decides to get up."

"You make my dick hard and now you want to talk, but okay." I could point out that he made his own dick hard, but I just let him continue. I didn't expect to hear what came next. Diesel's mood takes a one eighty and my heart breaks for him.

He tells me that when he was in high school, he couldn't do anything right in his father's eyes. Sevyn was the one who could do no wrong. He was made to feel like a fuck up and a failure because all he wanted to do was his music. Sevyn was the smart one, or so his father thought. He began grooming him in their high school years to join his company. Diesel finally moved out when he was seventeen and he was told not to come back. This broke his mother's heart.

Diesel and Sevyn knew they had to do something. Their mother wasn't taking her perceived loss of her son very well.

She had stopped eating and was depressed all the time. For the sake of preventing her from choosing between her son and her husband, the brothers became exact replicas of one another. Their father didn't even bat a lash at Sevyn changing his identity by getting tattoos. He just figured that it was part of him becoming a man and his need to find his own identity. Since Diesel was no longer in the house, he didn't know that he was getting the exact same tattoos. The haircuts and everything else identifiable needed to be an exact match. This allowed Diesel to substitute with his brother in and out of house without detection as long as he stayed out of their dad's way. Their mom wasn't thrilled when she found out what they had done, but it was done. They had to be very careful. Diesel finished his education online and stayed with friends who he could trust with their secret.

Their plan was supposed to be just for a little while, but then when their dad started grooming Sevyn to one day take over his acquisition and merger company, they formed a plan to bring Diesel in. Right now their father doesn't even acknowledge that he has two sons. Now that he is dying, the two of them are formulating a way for them to both be owners of the company before the plan can be blocked by the board.

Diesel recalls that part of his life, and I can see the pain in his eyes. I just want to hug him. I can't even imagine what that feels like—to not feel accepted or to have to change your identity in order to be allowed back into your home. It makes sense now why he is so reluctant to let people close to him.

"I'm so sorry you had to go through that, Diesel. That's awful." Sevyn nods in agreement.

"The times that I took Diesel's place in the house were

so that he could take mine in the company. I needed help with few projects and in turn, I helped him with some of his music. This also allowed us to test our detectability with everyone. Kind of like, on the job training. My brother truly has the intellect of a fucking genius. He deserves to be right next to me when we reveal the company has two new owners and not just one."

I'm so glad we're having this talk. Having this insight helps me to understand Diesel more. He's had to deal with shit no kid should ever have to go through. He just looks out the window now and I know our morning of flirtation is gone. He has a distant look in his eyes that I haven't seen before. I wish I could take him into the bedroom and make him forget—for now anyway. I hear footsteps and voices coming our way and that thought is now dead. He gets up and heads toward the back and I reach for him. Sevyn shakes his head so I pull my hand back.

"Don't," Sevyn warns. After Diesel is out of ear shot he tells me to give him space. "He just needs a minute. He'll come back when he's ready. He doesn't want any sympathy. It makes him feel weak. It took me a while to understand what he needs when he gets like this and the answer is nothing. He deals with it in his own way—a way that works for him." I nod, but it still breaks my heart. He was there for me when I was down, even though the reason was because of him. Now I feel like I'm just sitting here when he needs me. Lily and the guys join us at the table. I nibble at my food. I'm worried about Diesel. The bus slows to a complete stop and he is the first one off.

We've stopped so they could get a few things from the

store. The next stop on the tour is Las Vegas. I was tempted to tell Brooke to fly up for the weekend so we could gamble. We both have always wanted to go. Now I'm in a funk. I stay on the bus when everyone else gets off. I lay across my bunk and finally do the writing I was supposed to do this morning before I got distracted. So far I've only written about the two shows they've played and a behind the scenes account of what the guys do to get ready. I know I need something more—more insight.

DIESEL

I'm glad I got all of that out. I don't plan on telling that story again. Lourdes deserved to hear it for what I put her through, but I'm retiring that part of me as of now. I will take over Beck Investment Firm with Sevyn, because more than anything, that is what he wants. It's my restitution for the shit my father put me through. I just hope he lives long enough to learn that the son he wrote off is just as fucking capable as the one he put on a pedestal. That would make all this ten times more worth it. I'm a little thrown that Lourdes hasn't tried to talk to me all day, to be honest. I told her my life story. Something that, up until now, only Sevyn and I knew about. I didn't even tell the friends I was staying with at the time. Not all of it any-way—just need to know shit.

Well the main thing is I finally explained it all to her. I

hope she got what she needed. I hope she now knows that what we shared was real. It wasn't some game or sick joke Sevyn and I cooked up for the hell of it. She wasn't a pawn for our enjoyment. I can't make her care about my past. It's my cross to bear. Me reliving that fucking dark time of my life for her sake and her reaction, or lack thereof, is what I needed to move on. I've avoided her all afternoon and she didn't attempt to check on me.

I was a little jealous earlier when I came into the kitchen and saw my brother's hand on her. I had to show them both who had the power to make her melt. She tried to act unfazed, but I know I could fuck her with little effort if I wanted to. Thing is, she continues to be my weakness. The more I allow things to grow beyond platonic with her, the more I find myself going down the same path that I need to put a fucking road block on. I need to see what Ivy's up to. If she is down with just sex, then I may just be willing to hook up with her again. I could use the distraction. I'll see where her head is at later. Right now, I need to get ready. We go on stage in an hour.

"You ready, man?" Xander says taking a seat next to me.

"Why wouldn't I be? Fuck yeah, I'm ready." The extra enthusiasm is for his benefit. I know I'll snap out of whatever the hell this is the minute our music starts.

"Good. You just seemed a little out of it today. You didn't come out of that room all day. Just wanted you to know I was here if you needed to talk," he offers. "Oh, and thank you for being there for my sister. For some reason she reaches out to you more than she does her own brother." He chuckles, but he wouldn't be if he knew why.

I change the subject by discussing the need for some rehearsal time with Reckless Ambition before our next show. I still want to bring Ivy and Anderson in on a couple of our songs. I need to focus on some new songs too.

We talk until it's time for us to go on.

The lights dim and we take our places. Xander strums the first few chords before Gable joins in on drums. Keyser comes in with his guitar and the fucking crowd goes ape shit before the first lyric leaves my mouth. "One way or another, I'm going to find you," I begin. It's our rendition of Until The Ribbon Breaks' *One Way or Another*. The beat is sexy as fuck. I use its sensual undertones to seduce the audience. I pull my T-shirt over my head and run my hand down my abs. The response is fucking astounding. I decide to give them a show. I continue the lyrics while unbuttoning my jeans. I stroke my dick through my underwear, giving them a peek at the outline of my cock through my underwear. The women are eating it up. I bet I just made all their pussies wet with desire. It just so happens that I'm feeling a little bit generous. Maybe I'll let some lucky woman, or a few, get a taste. For now, that's all they get. I tuck my shit back into my jeans and zip them back up. I leave the button undone though. My guys give me a look of curiosity, but they don't miss a beat. You'd think my extra performance was part of the show. We continue the rest of our set with me shirtless and seducing the fuck out of the crowd. Our whole performance was one big act of foreplay and now I'm ready to sink my shit into some pussy. It's time to get back to being me.

CHAPTER
Ten

DIESEL

WE'RE BACK IN OUR DRESSING ROOM AND THE GUYS are giving me shit for my little ad lib tonight. Xander isn't too impressed, but Gable and Keyser don't give a shit. They think making women wet their panties can only be a good thing. They buy the fucking tickets. Men do too, but an abundance of women in one place is going to bring the men too. Lourdes and Lily are off in the corner talking about who knows what. I can't be worried about what she thought about tonight. There is a knock at our door and we all stop talking, wondering who it is. I get up and open the door. It's one of the security guys.

"Hey, man. I know Xander said to not let anybody back

here, but there is a woman up front that is insisting that she knows you," he says. So that's why we haven't been having any groupie action. Xander has been cock blocking his own boys. I can't help but laugh at his slick ass.

"Who is it? Did she give a name?" I look behind me and see that they're all listening.

"No. She says she'll only talk to you," the security guy explains. Well I'm not about to let some woman back here on her word. Not one that I haven't picked out as my fuck tonight.

"Take me to her," I say. I wonder who this mystery woman could be. Probably somebody I fucked and already moved on from. I'll give her a few minutes of my time but that's it.

I walk out with the security guy who has yet to give me his name. He is a few steps ahead of me for my protection. I see the blonde hair first and then the outline of her comes into focus. I stop a couple feet from her with a slack jaw. I'm not believing my fucking eyes right now.

"Hi, Diesel." She smiles. That fucking voice. It's been so long. Melissa sounds like a little girl, but she is all fucking woman. She's short, like Lourdes. They're even built the same. Tiny waist with a big ass and tits. The only other woman to fucking obliterate my heart is standing before me. Although she's never gotten as far as Lourdes, she's the one who introduced me to a world beyond Vanilla. You can't tell by looking at her, but she's even freakier than I am. My dick hardens from the memories. Unfortunately, I also remember than she walked away after she got bored with me. She needed someone more hardcore.

"What are you doing here, Melissa?" I ask, eager to get

straight to the point. Is it my inevitable fame that has brought her forward?

"Don't be like that. I just wanted to see you." Her smile is gone. I hate that her damn voice so damn cute.

"Why?" I push. She's going to have to give me more than that.

"Umm…" She looks down to the floor and my cock jumps at her submission. She is playing with me. She knows me in that sense better than anyone else. She knows what gets me going because she pulled this out of me. My demons were created by her. "I've missed you."

"No. Why are you here now?" I don't do vague.

"I didn't know how to find you before, after you left New York. I made a mistake, but when I came to find you, you had left. I heard about your band touring with Reckless Ambition on the radio and I knew I needed to come. I knew there was a chance you wouldn't see me, but I needed to say that I am sorry." She is still looking at the floor. "I'm not that same person from a few years ago Diesel. And if I had to guess, neither are you. I had to grow up—to find myself," she finishes.

There is some truth to what she is saying. I'm not that same naive fuck that she toyed with back then. That shit would never work with me now.

"So you've come and given your apologies. I accept. Now what?" It's a legitimate question. What did she hope to accomplish by coming here.

"I don't know. I didn't get that far. I wasn't even sure if you would agree to see me."

"Well, you kind of didn't give me much choice. It's not like you gave security your name." The security guy is standing over to the side, no doubt listening in on our conversation. She looks up at me finally.

"I'm sorry," she says and a lone tear trickles down her cheek. Damn her. She knows I don't like to be the reason for a woman's tears. That is why I try to be as upfront as I can.

I know I'm going to regret this, but I remove the rope so she can get through. I nod over at the security guy and walk her back to my dressing room. The guys have no idea who she is. I've never talked about her. Not even to Sevyn. When I left New York, she was dead to me. One thing all of this has shown me is that some people are worthy of redemption. Lourdes has forgiven Sevyn and I so maybe, if Melissa is being sincere, I can forgive her too. I'm trying to let our memorable moments outweigh the bad. She gave me an outlet—a sense of control. I was able to shed the weak boy that had been crushed by the disappointment of his father and transform to the man I am today. I owe her a chance to be redeemed for that reason alone. I'm not looking for another relationship because no woman will get that from me…maybe ever. I will spend some time catching up with her and maybe explore some of our mutual interests, but nothing more.

We enter the dressing room and the chatter stops. Melissa latches onto my arm and casts her eyes downward again. Shit, she's assumed the role of my submissive. She's falling back into how we were before she left. The guys don't know what to look for so I doubt they catch on. I look toward Lourdes, whose eyes are trained on her. She and I have never reached this level so I'm not sure if she recognizes what's going on.

"Stop," I whisper. "I'm not your Dom, and my band doesn't know that side of me, so you can't…" She seems to understand. She raises her head slowly, but doesn't let me go.

"Who do we have here, Diesel? I'm guessing this is the woman that the security guy was talking about," Keyser digs.

"Yes. This is Melissa. An old friend of mine." The girls walk up to get a better look at her. Lourdes has her arms folded. Her lips are tight. She doesn't like this one bit.

"And when he says friend, he means an old girlfriend," Melissa says timidly.

"An ex, huh?" Keyser says checking her out. "Damn, man." I know he likes what he sees. Melissa is dressed in skinny jeans, a tight cleavage showing T-shirt, and fuck-me stilettos.

"You voice is so cute," Lily comments. "I wasn't expecting such a cute squeaky voice coming from that package," she adds admiring Melissa's curves like Keyser.

"Diesel has never mentioned you," Xander admits before realizing his mistake. He face palms and Melissa lets out the most adorable giggle.

"No worries. Our break up wasn't the prettiest one. I was devastated to learn that he had moved before we could reconcile," she admits.

"So is that what you two are doing now? Reconciling?" Lourdes finally speaks up. That fucking question is loaded with sarcasm. She's pissed. Holy crap, how could the guys miss the jealous undertones? The room is shocked silent. Before Melissa can answer though, there is a quick knock on the door before Ivy barges in. The rest of her bandmates are right behind her.

This night just turned into a fucking hot mess in an instant. Melissa laces her small fingers through mine and I don't want to push her away. After all, Lourdes hasn't spoken to me all day after I spilled my damn heart to her and Ivy has been giving me the cold shoulder since she found me in a room held up with Lourdes. My life is a fucking soap opera right now.

The guys come in and take a seat after raiding our liquor stash. To say they are oblivious to the tension that has increased to nth degree since they walked in, is an understatement. Ivy walks over and stares daggers at Melissa. Her glacial concentration hasn't left our joined hands since she walked into the room. I feel it coming before it happens. I could predict it.

"You're Ivy St. Clair, right? Backup vocals for Reckless Ambition?" It's a rhetorical question since the band is pretty fucking famous. Melissa's attempt to diffuse the obvious anger radiating off of Ivy is an epic fail. She isn't even paying attention to Lourdes, even though when she was drunk she called Ivy a whore and rubbed in the fact that I was leaving with her.

"Obviously," Ivy spits. "Who the hell are you?" Now why in the hell is she jealous? I only fucked her one time. Thank God I didn't tap that more than once if this is how possessive she gets.

"Ivy, stop," I say but Melissa answers. I see the train wreck.

"I'm Diesel's ex," she answers. She tightens her grip and straightens a little taller. I can feel the hint of difference in her posture.

"Oh. Ex. As in insignificant," Ivy retorts. "I fucked him just a few days ago so I guess that makes me his ex too." She laughs condescendingly.

"Are you really comparing your ex fuck with our two year relationship?" She drops my hand. "Little girl, please. I'd run circles around you. You'd wish you knew half of what I knew in that department. Keep bragging cause if that pussy of yours was worth anything, we'd be having a different conversation. You wouldn't be bragging about having him a few days ago because he would have already been back balls deep in that. When we were together, he couldn't go a day let alone two or three." And there it is. The whole room is so quiet you could hear a damn pin drop. Melissa is what you call a switch. She can go from submissive to alpha in the blink of an eye. *Ivy meet Melissa's alpha.*

The evil smile she's sporting now is daring Ivy to do something.

"Whatever, bitch. Didn't seem that way when I was making him come."

"Okay. On that note, let's go," Xander says as he sees, like I do, where this is going. Lourdes spins on her heels and she is the first out the door. She doesn't wait on anyone.

"Damn man. I want to see a chic fight," Keyser grumbles. I push Melissa out the door while Ivy huffs.

"Silly girl. I hope you know that a dick doesn't need pussy to cum. Hell he can do that with a few strokes from his hand. Please don't let the natural result of friction against his cock be the indicator as to whether your shit was good or not. Small hint for you. If he can go without it, it probably wasn't."

I don't even know why I brought her back to the bus. I just needed to get her away from Ivy before things escalated. Melissa has a sharp tongue and an even bigger dominant personality. It really takes a bigger alpha to get her to submit—to top her. Thing is, I couldn't transition into the Dom in me that she listens to in front of everyone. That little show would have been over before it started. I could have silenced her with a single command.

When we get on the bus, the guys are already sharing the "almost cat fight" as they call it with Sevyn.

When he sees her, he drops the water bottle he's holding and water spills on the floor next to the sofa where he is siting. The guys scatter to avoid getting soaked by the water. Melissa goes statute still. I have to push her further into the living area before she snaps out of it. I forgot to tell her that I had a twin. It never came up. It was all too new—to fresh—to bring up at the time.

"Melissa. That is my brother, Sevyn," I say stating the obvious. She gives a slight wave but then turns to bury her face in my chest. It's endearing that she saves this vulnerable side for me. He waves back, but she's facing me now so she doesn't see.

"Man, this girl ripped Ivy a new one," Keyser continues the story.

"What time do you have to be back?" I ask Melissa.

"I'm off for a week," she admits. "I got a one-way ticket and left the return date open because I was unsure how tonight would go."

"So basically, you don't have to be back tonight?"

"No," she answers simply.

"That's all that I needed to know." We walk past Lourdes's bunk on the way to the bedroom and she doesn't even look up. She has her earphones in and she is typing away on her laptop. The small intake of breath lets me know that she sees us. Our unfinished business is inevitable, but for now she needs to explain a few things.

CHAPTER
Eleven

Lourdes

HAVEN'T HEARD BACK FROM BROOKE SINCE I TEXTED HER. My status of "holding up" has died a slow death. Knowing that his ex-girlfriend of two years is here, and that he invited her into our bubble, has set me back to the fucking stone ages. Realistically, I can't be jealous, but I am. Reality can fuck off. *Right off to be exact.* I'm not strong enough to battle my emotions. I'm fighting an uphill battle. There. Are. Two. Of. Them. Both are more assertive than me, so I'm sure they usually get what they want.

Last night I had to immerse myself in my writing to keep from flipping the fuck out. The rationales Melissa gave about Ivy being insignificant, apply to me too. He's flirted with me here and there, but nothing to indicate he was going through withdrawals from how good our sex was. He didn't even bother correcting her.

The bus is quiet now and I hate the insecure girl's flesh I'm wearing right now. Refusing to wallow in the self-pity I'm creating for myself, I get out of my bunk.

Although we haven't created a duty schedule for our chores, I figure I'll pull my weight by cooking breakfast for everyone. Nothing extravagant like Sevyn and Diesel, but on a scale of palatable to gourmet—edible. You can't screw up eggs right? I scramble eggs, and make grits and bacon. Now that their breakfast is ready, I want to try my hand at making poached eggs. I put water on the stove and add vinegar.

"Morning, Lourdes."

"Morning, Sevyn," I greet, turning to give him a once over, but he is covered up this time. I can't see if he has the tattoo or not. Only reason I can convincingly tell the two brothers apart now is because I'm sure Diesel is still making up for lost time with Melissa.

"Smile, beautiful," he encourages. "She's only here for a few days," he points out.

"I guess I'm being pretty transparent, huh?"

"Just a tad, but I'm here for you." I turn back toward the stove so he can't see the tears fall. I wipe them furiously with the back of my hand. We haven't even fucked since the lake house. Yet, here I am so jealous. I actually let out a breath when I see Lily and the guys come to investigate the smell permeating throughout the bus.

"Remember what I said," Sevyn says as he join the guys. He doesn't look back, but the words he left me with, calm my overactive mind, to a degree. Lily is the first to arrive in the kitchen so she can make a plate for Xander and herself. She must see my red, puffy eyes.

"Lourdes, can I ask you something?" she begins.

"Of course."

"Anything?" Okay now she is starting worry me.

"I would never say anything, but what is going on between you and Diesel, and don't say nothing," she pleads. She's promising not to spill the beans. I need to trust someone with my feelings, especially since Brooke has her own priorities to worry about. That sole proprietorship stake in our friendship is dwindling. I'm so proud of her.

"Okay. What do you want to know?" I lead off.

"Are you two now, or have you ever been, involved?" I can't believe I'm sharing with her.

"Yup," I answer simply.

"Oh, I am going to need more detail than that," she gushes.

"Not here," I say looking around the room until I spy the guys on the sofa. I'm hoping the guys hadn't tuned into her probing questions.

"Fine. Let's finish our breakfast and have some girl time on my bunk." I laugh because I'm not sure that spot is any better. Voices carry on this bus. I nod in agreement and we head to finish our breakfast with the guys.

I catch Sevyn looking over at me a few times. Melissa and Diesel finally come out of the room and I cringe seeing her wild bed hair. She's wearing one of his band tees and the tiniest shorts ever that don't even cover the bottom of her ass cheeks. It doesn't take a rocket scientist to figure out the night the two of them had. I feel a hand grip my knee under the table and realize it's Sevyn. I can feel the tears welling in my eyes. I need to move before they fall.

"Hmmm. What is that, smelling so yummy?" Melissa asks prancing her ass into the kitchen with Diesel in tow. Unlike Sevyn, he can't even look at me. Xander tells her that I made breakfast, but it feels like my head is underwater. Everything sounds muffled. I'm in a vortex of emotions spinning out of control.

I push back from the table and plaster a fake smile on my face. "I'm going to hit the shower now that the room is free," I say casually to Lily. I feel anything but. She nods and I take my plate to the kitchen. I walk right past Melissa and Diesel, but I avoid eye contact with them both. Once I reach the shower and turn it on, I allow myself to have the meltdown that has been building. I remove my clothes and literally crawl in. I let the water run over me as I hunch over in a ball. I've never felt so lost as I do in this moment—so broken. I don't have anything left with Diesel so I can't even be mad. No, my inner turmoil is not from anger, it's from the constant feeling of emptiness. A feeling of merely existing when life is happening all around me. The feeling of never being quite good enough. The world's punching bag. I have no fight left and I just want to leave now. I don't know what I was thinking. I can't do this.

I feel this bus slow to a stop, but I don't move from this spot. I can faintly make out Diesel and Melissa's voices over the water. Apparently they've come to get clothes and whatever else before getting off the bus.

"I still can't believe you came all this way and didn't

bring luggage," Diesel laughs.

"I wasn't sure if I'd be turning right back around," she explains.

"Well, we can get you something when we get off the bus."

"Sounds like a plan," she agrees.

And then they're gone. "Lourdes?" I hear Lily call for me from the other side of the door. "Can I come in?" She doesn't even get ready in this bathroom, so I know she's just checking on me.

"I'm showering now, Lil. I'll catch up with you later," I say trying to force the words past the lump in my throat.

"Um okay. I hope we get a chance to have that talk." The closing of the bedroom door tells me that I'm alone again. I wish this water could wash away everything I'm feeling right now. I don't know how long I've been sitting on the floor of the shower. The hot water is long gone. The shower door creaks open, but I don't even look up.

"Lourdes. Come on." Strong hands reach in to pull me out. Instinctively I know that it is Sevyn. I don't even resist. My whole body is limp from being on the shower floor so long. He just wraps me in a towel and carries me into the room. He tries to sit me on the bed, but I claw at him and hold on for dear life. He must understand that I don't want to be on the bed that he shared with her. He walks me over to the chair in the corner instead.

"Where are your clothes?" he asks.

"Closet," I say, pointing to the open closet next to me.

He pulls out sweats. He dresses me in them, forgoing any bra or underwear. I don't even care that he's seeing me naked right now. I don't care about anything. I'm just here.

"We're getting off this bus," he informs. I shake my head but he continues right on by putting shoes on me. "I wasn't asking, darling."

The change in his voice—the firmness—snaps me to attention. He can't be…could he? I can't explain it, but Diesel's voice dips into a different octave when his inner Dom comes out. Are he and Sevyn similar in this way too? It's not like I can ask without potentially giving away Diesel's secret. Once I'm dressed, he links his fingers through mine and pulls me up. An electric current shoots through my body. I welcome the feeling. It's a pleasant contrast to the numbness. When we get off the bus, Sevyn doesn't let go of my hand.

"Where to first?" he asks.

"I don't know. This was your idea," I point out. "My vote would have been to stay on the bus."

"Sorry, but self-pity isn't an option today. Now you don't have to like it, but I'm rescuing you." He begins walking and it looks like I have no choice but to keep up.

"Rescue me from what?" I challenge.

"From yourself," Sevyn answers without hesitation. I can't argue with that. Solitude would have just given me more time to overthink shit and fall deeper into sadness.

We spent the entire day goofing off after he found out that the bus wasn't moving until later this afternoon. He took me to some arcade and we challenged each other on various games. I was surprised that I was even able to laugh. He pretended to be a sore loser, but I think he was letting me win.

We had lunch, walked the streets of Nevada, played games, and finally ended up at a movie theater. His phone went off a few times, but he sent it to voicemail every time.

"Do the guys know where we are? They're not waiting for us to leave are they?" Is that what the missed calls are for?

"No. I messaged them and told them you were with me. Xander already told me what time we needed to be back." The new X-Men movie is out so we decide to get tickets to that. Sevyn has been great at distracting me today or "rescuing" me as he calls it. He's been a perfect gentleman too. Once we're in our seats, I realize that our hands have been intertwined all day, aside from the time I was kicking his ass at video games. This is a change of pace from today's playful activities. This is more intimate. He pulls me a little closer and I take in the scent of his cologne. He smells really good. There is a seat handle between our two seats that keeps me from snuggling closer. The theater begins to fill, but in this moment it's just us.

"Thank you for today," I say softly, even though movie trailers are playing and the actual movie haven't started yet. He leans closer and I don't move. His lips find mine and he kisses me gently at first. He takes his hand from mine to cup behind my neck. He deepens the kiss and I swear my panties are soaked within seconds. I open for him and he takes my mouth with such conviction. I run my hands down his chest and he growls. He pulls back and I instantly feel bereft.

My lips tingle from his assault. Holy shit this man can kiss. He's fucking amazing at this rescuing thing. His hooded lids tells me he felt it too.

He jumps up all of sudden and pulls me with him. He takes me to an empty corridor and boosts me up so that my legs can wrap around his waist. He pushes my back against the wall and palms my ass while he takes my mouth again. I can feel the hardness of his dick through my sweats. I shamelessly rub myself against it as I suck on his tongue. I'm dizzy with how good this feels. I feel my orgasm building and I'm powerless to stop it. He pushes me further against his erection and I come undone. When I stop moving, he just smiles.

"I need to use the ladies room." I feel my cheeks heating. I'm sure my face is turning red.

"I bet," he smirks. "Was it good for you?" I cover my eyes but he removes my hands. I look down to see the hard imprint of his cock against his jeans.

"I'll be back," I say as he lets me go. He winks and I head down the hall to find a bathroom. I'm not wearing any panties, and my pussy is soaked. I can't believe that just happened. And in a public place where we could have been caught. I don't know what came over me.

For the duration of the movie, Sevyn doesn't make any attempt to hold my hand again. When it's over, we start our ten-minute trek back to the bus. He is noticeably quiet and it makes me feel like I did something wrong.

"Can you just say something? Are you upset with me?" I finally ask.

"No. Why would I be mad at you?" He shoves his hands in his pockets and looks off into the distance. His words are filled with remorse so I probe further.

"You haven't said more than two words at a time since I…since I did that to you," I point out.

"I made a mistake, Lourdes." He lets out a long sigh. "I shouldn't have kissed you, and I damn sure shouldn't have taken you into that hallway. I started it all, not you."

"So I'm a mistake?" I ask shocked.

He winces at my words. "You're not a mistake. My actions were. I took advantage of your vulnerability. It's not me that you want. I think you and I both know that."

"Please save me the 'it's not you, it's me' bullshit." I stop in the middle of the sidewalk. We're getting closer to the bus and I'm not ready to go back. "Fucking thanks. Now that I've managed to be rejected by both brothers, my day is complete." People go around us. I'm pretty sure I look like a crazy person, but I don't care.

"Will you just stop? That's not what I'm doing at all. I think you are a gorgeous woman. If circumstances were different, you couldn't keep me from pursuing you. I can't have you so it was wrong to…" His voice trails off.

"Whatever, Sevyn. No worries. I don't need your 'let her down easy' speech. We did nothing wrong. Diesel made it clear that he's not interested in having anything other than a friendship with me. He reiterated that fucking point when he brought his ex onto the bus and banged her damn brains out in the very room where he spent the day before with me."

"Lourdes, the fact that you were once his means you could never be mine. You weren't just some woman in his life. He made you his girlfriend and that's pretty fucking significant. He doesn't do relationships. You and Melissa were his only two exceptions. Regardless of the wall he has up now, you meant something to him." He looks off again. He pauses for a brief second before he continues. "The mistake is not you. The mistake was letting what I was feeling cloud what I know to be wrong. He is who you want, but you settled for me because of our resemblance. I'm sorry."

"Just forget it. It was a slip. We'll leave it that and pretend it never happened." I start walking again. I can't get away from his regret fast enough. It makes me feel pretty shitty. I know what he said was legitimate. Surely it goes against some kind of bro code to mess with your brother's ex-girlfriend. It was still nice to feel wanted for a little while.

I'm the first to board the bus with Sevyn only steps behind me. It's nearly five in the afternoon. Xander and Lily are vegging out, watching reality TV. Xander tells us we're rolling out in an hour and that everyone else is off taking a nap in the bunks. Sevyn walks past us and announces he is going to go take a nap as well.

"Did you enjoy your time out?" Xander asks. Lily eyes me closely. I was supposed to have some girl talk with her and I pushed her away earlier. "Sevyn messaged me and told me that since everybody had kind of paired off that he was just going hang out with you for the day." *Great.* Now I feel like I was a project that was the last one picked.

"We had a blast. It has been a long time since I could act like a kid and play arcade games." I only tell him about part of our outing for obvious reasons. "I guess I'll take nap too. It's been a long day."

"Okay. Glad you had fun," he assures.

"Will talk with you later, Lil," I say so she knows that I'll fill her in later.

CHAPTER
Twelve

DIESEL

WHEN I WAKE UP THE ROOM IS COMPLETELY DARK. I don't have to turn the light on to know that I'm alone in bed. I can hear the guys talking on the other side of the door and I smell chicken. I live on that shit so I can pick that scent out with ease. Maybe Sevyn is taking pity on my diet. That fucker is a master in the kitchen and I could never resist his cooking. I flip the light on and look for a t-shirt to throw on with my shorts.

I guess Melissa is out there. She has been surprisingly different these last couple of days—attentive. She didn't even get upset when I told her I didn't want to just jump back into how we left things. I don't know what has come over her. She's my match with the kinky shit that I'm into. I wouldn't have to instruct her on what I like or test her boundaries. We just complement each other sexually. This was my chance to have the kinky sex I've had to restrain from, yet I just couldn't go there. Something is holding me back. Melissa was understanding and told me she's just happy I let her apologize. I gave her one of my shirts last night after her shower because she didn't bring any clothes, but I'm sure the entire bus thinks we fucked. Truth is, we spent time catching up. There were guys that she thought she could move on with, but none of them were me. I even told her the damn story of my life that I promised myself I would never tell again. Unlike Lourdes, I felt like she really listened. She was the comfort that I needed. Ironic that she was the reason I found a way to take back control when I needed an outlet.

I'm almost out of the bedroom when I hear the music cranked up to ignorant levels. Paula Cole's *Where Have All the Cowboys Gone?* What the hell? We've been on the road for a week now and this is the first time we've played any music. Then I hear her. "*I will do the laundry, if you pay all the bills,*" Lourdes sings. I've heard her sing once before, but shit she's got some pipes. Her back is to me and she has one of our cordless mics up to her mouth. I'm so enthralled with her singing, it takes me a second to realize Melissa is watching my reaction from the kitchen. She isn't seated around the living room like everybody else who's enjoying Lourdes's performance. I go to her and she hands me a plate of baked chicken breast and brussel sprouts.

"I cooked for you," she says. I see the question in her eyes. "I remember you like to eat healthy. Keyser fried some chicken, but I thought I should make sure you had yours baked." I pull her into a hug.

"It seems like our guests are doing more cooking than we are," I joke. "Seriously, though. Thank you for looking out for me, Melissa." I take my food over to the table and she follows me.

"So she can sing, huh?" She points toward Lourdes who is now sitting next to Xander.

"Yeah. She's pretty good. What are they doing?"

"They're having some sort of karaoke night. They're drawing names. Whoever draws your name gets to pick which song you're going to sing," She says, explaining their little game.

"Why aren't you playing?" I ask in between bites.

"One, I can't sing and two, I didn't feel like it." I nod my understanding and some time passes before she continues.

"Do you like her?" Should have seen that one coming.

"Who?" I ask, knowing damn well where she's going with this.

"The girl singing...Lourdes, I think is her name?"

"No. She's Xander's sister. He'd kick my ass." My answer is partly true at least. Melissa rolls her eyes and shoves me lightly.

"I wouldn't doubt that, but that doesn't mean you don't want to fuck her. Is she the reason you're holding back with us?" I stop eating and give her my full attention. She needs to know I'm serious.

"Melissa, there is no *us*. I haven't done anything with you because I don't want you to misinterpret what's going on here. It was great catching up last night, but you can't just undo everything with one visit and think things are just going to resume where they left off. At this point in my life, I'm not looking to be in a relationship with anybody. I'm sorry if you got the wrong impression." The disappointment is evident. I'm so glad I didn't let my dick take the lead on this one. I already hurt Lourdes, and maybe even Ivy. This is a prime example of why I need to keep my shit away from people I will have to deal with regularly. Feelings get involved and it's messy.

"No need to explain, Diesel. I get it. I gave my apology, you accepted, that's all that I can ask for. I didn't get on this bus to be your fuck either. I'll be getting off once the bus stops again and getting a return plane ticket home. I wish you the best." She goes to get up, but I put a hand over hers.

"Still friends?" I don't want to unravel the process that we've made at mending things.

"Of course we are. You can't get rid of me in your life that easily. I'll stay in touch," she promises.

"You better," I warn jokingly. "Hang with me tonight. We'll watch shit TV again in the room. Nothing more. Just enjoying each other's company for one more night before you leave." She agrees so I finish my dinner and bring her back to the room with me.

"Surprised you don't still have your game," she mentions. It's been forever since I've fucking played but I do have it. I'm the only gamer out of us all, but I rarely get to play anymore.

"Just you wait." I go to the closet and rummage through my shit until I come across my PS4 and the Tekken fighting game she used to like to play. When she sees it, she squeals and grabs it from me.

"I can't believe you still have this. You bought this for me remember? You're such a little thief."

"Whatever. You ready to get your ass handed to you?" I used to always let her win. Tonight I'll let her win sometimes. She need to get ready for my ninja moves.

"Memory serves me correctly, I was the one doing all the ass kicking." She giggles at that. She has no idea. I'm going to have to teach her a lesson. While I set the game up, she leaves to go get us drinks. Cucumber sparkling water to be exact. I don't really need the frou frou shit, but I'll indulge her. We play until neither of us can keep our eyes open.

I lost track of how many times I kicked her ass, but she managed to pull out some wins here and there. She's definitely gotten better since the last time we played. I turn off the game and pull the covers back so we can get further into the bed. She wraps her arms around me and I let her cuddle. She's shown a different person from the girl who walked away from me. I will hold onto this memory instead of the tarnished one. With redemption, comes peace.

Lourdes

Diesel only came out to eat last night before he went back into the room with Melissa. I watch her cater to him with her cooking. They look so cute together. Last night I heard laughter, and what sounded like video games, coming from the room until I finally dozed off. He was never that way with me and it makes me even sadder. I realize I never had his heart the way she apparently still does. It's time I accept the truth. Things will never be the same. He came into my life at a time when I needed someone to get through to me. I don't know if I could have come out of my introverted shell without him. Lord knows Brooke tried. I need to be productive today and start organizing some of these notes. I grab my laptop and head to the living area. Xander and Lily are doing their own thing, as usual. Doing a cross word puzzle from what I can tell. I don't see Gable or Sevyn and I'm guessing Diesel is still in the room with Melissa. Keyser walks into the room, coming from the front of the bus.

"Finally." He claps his hands in excitement. "Listen up. Tonight our asses will party. Gus says we'll be arriving in Phoenix in an hour. We'll be staying there for a couple days so Anderson rented a mansion. He's using his hook up to get the word out that we're having a fucking party tonight. Only people who have gotten any ass are you and Diesel," he says pointing at Xander.

"Settle down, Keyser. We need to find time to rehearse too. The concert is tomorrow night and we haven't had a chance to work with Reckless Ambition on what songs we'll bring them in on."

"Yeah, we can do that tomorrow morning. We know our shit. Tonight, we party. We have been boring as shit. I'm ready to cut loose for a bit." Keyser does a little dance. He's already in party mode. "Finally," he says again, more to himself.

"Let's at least have a meeting. We need to discuss new songs and see if Diesel has written anymore," Xander suggests. "Let's go tell him we need the room." The door opens at that moment and Diesel walks into the living area.

"Where's my brother?" he asks looking around.

"He's up front talking with Gus," Keyser tells him. He fills him in on the party tonight and Xander's request for a band meeting.

"Sure, man," Diesel says turning to Xander. "Melissa is in the shower right now and I need to speak to my brother real quick. After that, let's do it." Xander gives him the thumbs up from the sofa. Diesel grabs his brother from the front and then they go into the bedroom and shut the door.

DIESEL

"Hey man, just wanted to hash out this plan of yours. Sorry just seems like we could never get any alone time with the concerts and old flames showing back up in my life," I laugh. "I know you have to get back to New York tomorrow."

"Yeah, I booked my return flight this morning. It's was nice just to enjoy my visit with you and the guys without the weight of business on our shoulders my entire visit."

"True," I agree. "So what's this plan you had?"

"Well, our father signed over his shares to me before I contacted you. The cancer has spread and it's just a matter of time. He's been away from the office a lot to keep people from realizing he's sick. The board members and shareholders think he is just staying away to give me the space I need to thrive. I'm his protégé and they know he's grooming me to take over the company."

"So, this is a good thing. You already had your own shares is in the company so with his shares, you should have controlling interest now." I guess I don't understand what the problem is.

"I wish it was that simple, Diesel. Dad had fifty-one percent of the controlling shares and issued me nine percent when he brought me on. The purpose was to give us a combined sixty percent because certain decisions, especially major decisions, require a ten percent margin of a majority vote. His fifty one percent wouldn't be enough if the other forty-nine percent opposed a proposal." Sevyn takes a seat on the bed and the bouncing of his knee indicates he doesn't think I'll like what comes next.

"Just give me the bad news, Sevyn."

"Well, I think our father went to London to offer Morgan Investments a stake in the company. If he does that, he would have to offer them my original nine percent of shares since he can't take them from the other shareholders. I'd still have the fifty-one percent, but now if this Morgan person decides to band together with the other shareholders once our secret comes out, they win. We will be blocked from automatically bringing you onboard. We'd be at their mercy to decide your fate within the company, if at all," he says.

"Why would Claude do that? He had to know that it was a possibility they could join forces against you." I shake my head. Even with death at the door, he still manages to fuck me.

"He doesn't know about our plan Diesel. He doesn't know that I plan on giving you equal shares so we can run the company together. To him, it's a last ditch effort to ensure that I'll be okay—that I won't get in over my head. I'm sure he thinks he's giving Morgan Investments just enough shares to have an obligation to make sure that we don't go under, while not giving them enough to have any real power." He takes a deep breath and then blurts out his plan. "We need to come forward now."

"What?" I yell. "Why?"

"We need to leak that he's sick and that he may be potentially trying to bring another person on board to help run the company in his absence. That part is not true, but will get the shareholders all riled up. They'll block the addition of any new members."

"Don't you already have the sixty percent of the shares right now? He hasn't given away your original nine percent yet, has he?" I'm pacing now.

"No. I have the sixty percent controlling shares for now. Father hasn't announced that to the board either, but we've already signed the necessary paperwork with his attorney." He looks down to the floor. "I know what you're suggesting Diesel and I can't do it. I can't be the person to block his request to add an additional member. That would be the ultimate betrayal after he literally handed me over his controlling interest. If we leak information about his health and his intent to bring in a foreign partner, we won't have to get our hands dirty. I won't have to feel the guilt—his hurt from knowing this blow came from the son he trusted. Please Diesel. I want more than anything to share this company with you, but not like this."

I see the tears threatening to fall from my brother's eyes.

Personally, I don't give a shit, but I'll go along with his plan. He doesn't want to be the one to hurt Claude—at least have him know where this plan of deceit stemmed from. When he finally passes, he wants it to be on good terms.

"Fine, Sevyn. I'm sure you know how I feel about it. He didn't give me any consideration, but whatever. When is the leak supposed to happen?"

"Well, he's not due back until next Friday, so a couple days before that. Too soon and he'll speculate how it got out. Give it some time for him to be seen in London, so it can be generalized that the pieces were put together from his trip."

"Okay," I agree. The shower shuts off and I remember that Melissa is in there. I don't think she overheard anything. She walks out in a towel and nearly jumps out of her skin when she sees Sevyn. She looks between us to try to figure which brother is which.

"Sorry. I didn't know anyone was in here." She inches back until she's back in the bathroom. She closes the door, leaving a small gap. "Diesel can you hand me my clothes from the bag of stuff I bought yesterday?" When I step forward, she smiles so I guess she figured which brother was the correct one.

"We'll be arriving in Phoenix in less than an hour," I inform her. I would suggest that she delay her flight to attend the party tonight, but it's time I get back to my playboy ways. Keep it moving. Besides this is my last night to hang out with my brother. I need to get him out of his own head. He needs to be focused when he goes back to New York tomorrow.

"Okay. I'll be ready," she promises. Sevyn and I head back into the living area. The guys agree to just have a quick meeting in here since Melissa is getting dressed in the bathroom anyway. I have two new songs that I've been working on that are almost done. We discuss which song Ivy will sing with me and which song Anderson will join me on. It's still our set so we don't want them to overshadow our entire performance. Two songs for our collaboration is enough. We are able to wrap up our meeting rather quickly so we spend the rest of the time talking about the party tonight. Keyser and Gable are more excited than the rest of us. I can admit that we haven't exactly been living the life of rockers since we've gotten on the road. They're ready to let their hair down, figuratively speaking, and frankly so am I.

CHAPTER
Thirteen

Lourdes

OUR BUS ARRIVES AT A GORGEOUS MANSION AND I'M IN awe. The exterior is so grand and breathtaking. We pull around the circular drive before the bus comes to a stop. Reckless Ambition's bus is already here. I snap pictures of this place as soon as my feet touch the ground. I send them to Brooke via text. I miss her like crazy, but she hasn't been messaging me back. I hope she responds soon because I'm starting to worry.

"Look at this place," Lily says looping her arm through mine.

"I know, right?"

"Life of the rich and famous, baby," Keyser shouts. "Let's

do this. Bring on the women." We all giggle. Gable mockingly slaps him in the back of the head.

We all head into this palace, except Diesel and Melissa. Another car pulls up and he's handing her bags to the driver. So apparently she's leaving. I can't say that I'm sad to see her go. It doesn't change anything between Diesel and I, but at least I don't have to witness their connection in contrast to our lack thereof.

Lily grabs my hand. "Come on. Our first stop is the pool, woman."

"In January?" It's in the sixties here in Phoenix, but still. Not exactly pool weather. The wind is kind of snippy too.

"Indoor pool, crazy. Xander already scoped it out when he looked over the floor plan. And it's heated," she informs me. I guess I could use some pool time. Sounds fun. We find ourselves in one of the bedrooms upstairs to change. I swear it's the size of a small house. The closet is the size of a living room. What I wouldn't give to own a place like this…shit, just to live in a place like this.

I pull out the red bikini Brooke picked for me when we went shopping before I left. I change in the closet surrounded by mirrors. There is no way I can miss all the ass I have hanging from these string bikini bottoms. I tug at them, but it's no use. The triangle top gives me a little more coverage, but not a ton. I feel like I could be one of those women in the music videos with all my goods on display. I'm contemplating changing into the one piece I snuck into my suitcase. It's black and has its own skirt attached. Lily walks into the closet wearing a red bikini with black paisleys.

"Look at us. We match," she squeals. "I have to say, yours

is smoking hot. Wait until Diesel sees you." *Wait...What?* I was about to tell her I was thinking about changing, but she caught me off guard with that statement.

"Who said anything about Diesel? Who care what he thinks?" I retort.

"Girl, please. *You* care, and we will be talking about just how much by the pool. You're not getting out of our girl talk this time." I tug at my bottoms and look in the mirror with a frown. "Oh, come on. I see you're looking and having seconds thoughts. You look great so no changing." She pulls me toward the door before I can object. When we get to the indoor pool, everyone else is already there—both our guys and Reckless Ambition. I guess we took too long admiring that to die for room. I walk closely behind Lily, trying not to pay attention to the stares I'm getting.

"Damn, Lourdes. You've come a long way babe. That fucking bikini is—" Keyser looks over at Xander and decides not to finish that remark. He misses the scowl that Diesel is giving him.

"Doesn't she look fab?" Lily twirls me around and I could strangle her. I'm trying deflect the attention away from me. I catch the eye roll of Ivy and it kind of makes the attention worth it—just a little. I sit in the nearest chaise lounge chair, which just happens to be next to Diesel. Lily takes the one on the other side of me. Too late to change places with her without making a scene. Music starts playing overhead and I'm happy for the reprieve. In an instant, the roofing retracts, leaving just glass to surround us. It's then that I realize that this is a solarium. The sunlight filters in and now you can see the lush gardens outside as well as a second, outdoor, pool.

This place is magnificent.

A couple of wait staff enter with beer and cocktails. The pre-party has officially started. I luck out and get one of the few mojitos they have available. It's one of my favorites. Cool and refreshing, perfect for that quick buzz. I lean back in my chair and sip on my drink. I can feel Diesel's eyes on me, but I try to ignore it. It really is unfair that one look from him can get my blood boiling. But just because Melissa is gone now, does not mean I'm up for going back to being his play toy.

"I think I like this new bold you," Diesel says where only I can hear. I do look over at him now and he takes a sip of some kind of brown liquor in a glass.

"What are you talking about, Diesel?"

"Red is my favorite color, you know?" He takes another sip of his drink. He's already toying with me.

"Yeah. Mine too. I wonder what Melissa's favorite color is." I can play his game. One point for me.

"Black. Her favorite color is black. There's something about red, though. Sort of like when the color red is waved in front of a bull," he surmises.

"What's your point, *Diesel*?" He's talking in circles and I don't know his angle.

"You walk in here with all that ass barely covered by that string bikini and it's taking the will of a saint not to do something about it." I look around, but nobody is listening to us.

"Don't worry. I have enough will for the both of us. I'm sure those bed sheets aren't even cold yet from you and Melissa, yet here you are making sexual advances on me. You're such a manwhore." There I said it. He's been with Ivy, he's made moves to be with me, he had Melissa, and now he's trying to circle back to me. We haven't even been on the road a month yet. And my tingling girly parts are stupid as shit, so I choose to ignore her horny ass.

"*Mmm-hmm*, maybe," he admits. "But an honest one. Everybody I get involved with knows the score up front." He winks at me and finishes his drink. He signals the waiter over for a refill. I finish my drink off so that I can get another as well.

"We all have needs, Lourdes. I'm just honest about mine." He pulls his shirt over his head and I try not to melt in a puddle from his exposed abs that are so fucking taut and lickable. I swear I drink my second mojito in three swallows. Things are heating up. I can feel my skin flush. I know better, yet my body aches for him. I'm under his scrutiny. He watches as I reposition myself on the chair.

"Yeah, you're pretty honest about it. We all are witness to your whore parade," I say trying to verbally remind myself why my pussy shouldn't be on fire right now.

"I didn't fuck Melissa, Lourdes," he volunteers.

"I didn't ask if you did," I quip.

He narrows his eyes. "I know. I just needed to set the record straight. Not that it matters. Just want to put that out there. Never assume you know shit." He smirks. He's right. It doesn't matter so why does my heart feel a little relieved? I raise my empty glass for another drink, but he waves the guy off.

"No," he says firmly. *What the fuck?*

"No, what? You can't cut me off," I whisper hiss. He motions the guy over and I think he's about to tell him to get me my drink.

"Two waters, please." He smiles, but I'm not amused. The guy nods and hand him the two waters. "You need to drink water in between drinks and slow the hell down. We have a long night ahead with the party. At this rate, you'll be drunk off your ass before it begins."

"Not your problem now, is it?" I snap. How dare he try to cut me off!

"I beg to differ, sweetheart, since I was the one cleaning vomit off you and taking care of you all night the last time you over indulged." He stares at me, daring me to try to dispute that fact. He has a point, but damn if it doesn't still piss me off. I fold my arms and he laughs so loudly, we get some stares.

"Shut it. Okay fine. I'll drink the damn water. Give it to me." Our fingers brush as he passes it to me and it awakens the fucking tingles in my vagina that were lying dormant after he cut my alcohol off, fooling me into believing I had gotten that shit under control.

"Come on. No pouting babe. You know I'm only looking out for you." Hearing him call me babe is a mind fuck. I know that he's no good for me. I really need to move the fuck on. He's going to crush me. He's admitted over and over again, both through words and actions, that he is not interested in having anything with anybody. Just fucking. Yet he calls me baby or babe and my stupid as shit heart skips a beat, like it's oblivious to the facts.

I chug the water because I will not react to his endearment. Every time he uses babe, baby, sweetheart, or any other word in his manwhore repertoire, I need to replace it with fuck buddy. I need to be realistic and not be sucked in by his charms.

"I'm going to rehearse with the guys. Remember what I said. Take it easy, babe," he says, getting up from his chair. *Fuck buddy* I say to myself. I wave and watch the sexiness of his back as he retreats. He says a few words to Xander and they round up the rest of the band members. They all head back into the main part of the house so that just leaves Lily and myself. I know what this means. *Girl talk time.* They're barely out the door before she scoots her chair closer to mine.

"Okay. Spill, woman," she says. I laugh because I called it. I knew she was bursting at the seams to find out about Diesel and me.

"What do you want me to tell you?" I tease her. She looks ready to stab me.

"Tell me all about you and Diesel. I know there is history between the two of you. You admitted as much, but then you left me hanging. I didn't push because you had a few mopey days and I guessed it was because of the addition of ass he brought onto the bus, and Ivy."

"Pretty accurate," I admit. I didn't plan on going into great detail about our history, but Brooke has been missing in action and I could use a friend to talk to. It sucks to hold all this in. "You first have to promise that you will never share any of this with Xander," I warn.

"I would never betray your trust like that Lourdes. Whatever you tell me will stay between us," she promises.

I believe her and it's comforting that I can trust her. I start from the beginning when I first met Diesel and how I wanted to stay away from him because I knew he was a manwhore. I tell her about Brooke, the rape, me falling for Diesel, our relationship, and finally the deceit. I tell her how my world was shattered to learn he had a twin. One that I had spent time with, but not sexually. I explain that he has redeemed that part of our past, but I wouldn't divulge what Diesel shared with me when he, his brother, and I had that talk. That's not my story to tell. All she needs to know is that they had a reason for the switch and that I have forgiven them.

"Holy shit, girl." She shakes her head. "Had no idea you were dealing with so much." She gets up and hugs me and tears threaten to fall.

"Yeah. It actually feels good to let that all out. So you can see why I've been so emotional lately. I know I need to move on, but a part of me is still holding on to the time we had when things were good. He let me in once and now that is not even a possibility."

"I know it's hard. Thing is, you can't keep holding on by yourself. If it was just sex, that's one thing. You have real feelings for him still, so unless those feelings are mutual, you're setting yourself up to be crushed."

She's not telling me anything I don't already know. I nod in agreement. "Come on. Let's go plan what we're wearing tonight. You just need to meet your next distraction. Things will get better, but it's just going to take time. Even more time because you're seeing him every day on this tour."

"I know. Yeah come on. I have a nice buzz and I don't want to ruin it with thoughts of Diesel."

We head to the bus first to get some clothes to choose from. We're surprised to see Sevyn sitting in the living area flipping through channels. I assumed he went to rehearsal with the guys. He looks up at us when we board the bus and gives us a sexy smile.

"Hello, distraction," Lily says too faintly for him to hear. I laugh my ass off as we head to the closet in the bedroom.

"Uh no. You're crazy!" Okay I kind of omitted the freaky part of the afternoon I spent with Sevyn. Ending result being he rejected my ass. "From what I overheard from the guys, he's leaving tomorrow anyway."

"I guess it would have been pretty fucked up anyway. Regardless of Diesel's stance of no longer wanting a relationship, I think he would flip his shit if you banged his brother. You don't want to come between two brothers. Pay me no mind," she giggles. "I have lapses in judgment sometimes."

"So do I, apparently." I nod in agreement. If she only knew the truth behind that statement. Hopefully the day at the movie theater will stay between Sevyn and I.

We ended up not going back into the house before the party. Lily told me about her life back home, the classes that she's taking this semester, and her career goals. Thank God you don't get much work the first couple weeks of online classes, aside from reading, because neither of us has cracked open a book. After we get back on the road, we need to remedy that. The book I'm working on and my online classes can be the distraction, *hopefully.*

Lily turns on some music to get us in party mode and it works to rid some of the weight from our earlier heavy conversation. I find myself dancing to the beat. I'm not sure of how to dress for something like this, but I'm going with classy and not the obvious slutty choice. I'm sure there will be a few thirsty ones, but this a celebrity party. The desperation to be seen should be at a minimal, right?

"Ooh, that one," Lily says eyeing the dress I have in my hand. I was thinking the same thing. It's perfect and it just happens to be red. It's a Herve Leger cross chest strap bandage dress. It forms a keyhole between my breasts so they are slightly on display without being overly so. I don't have many expensive purchases, but this is one of them. It makes me feel sexy and that is what I'll need tonight, being surrounded by all the gorgeous women who can buy their beauty.

"I agree. I've never really had an occasion to wear her out," I say giving my dress an identity. "I'm going to pair it with my nude stilettos."

CHAPTER
Fourteen

Lourdes

"I wish I owned a dress like that," Lily admits. "I'm going go with my black sequin strapless tube dress with silver pumps." She holds the dress up and I nod my head in agreement.

"That will be super hot on you."

"Thanks. I'm going for sexy not slutty." She grins. *My sentiments exactly.*

"Same," I agree.

I use the shower first after laying my dress on the bed. When I come out, I get the shock of my life. I let out a deafening scream and then the tears start. I can't help it. Brooke is standing in the center of the bedroom and from the looks of it, she's dressed for the party. She's wearing an electric blue bandage dress and looks fabulous.

"I can't believe you're here," I say giving her the tightest hug ever. Lily stands off to the side, just smiling.

"Oh my gosh, how rude of me? Brooke you remember Lily, right?"

"Of course. We had a chance to get reacquainted while you were in the shower, too." Lily walks up to me and hugs me too before going to take her shower. I turn my attention back to Brooke.

"What are you doing here? How did you know where we'd be?" I fire so many questions at her. "Why didn't you return my calls? I was worried about you!"

"Slow down, chica," she giggles. "One question at a time. Diesel called me. He said he got my number from your phone. He knew you were missing me and wanted me to join you guys for a weekend. He paid and arranged everything. He sent a car to pick me up from the airport."

That is seriously the sweetest thing anyone has ever done for me. Diesel went to great lengths to set up a surprise visit from my best friend and I couldn't be happier. Shit like this makes it even more difficult to move on from him.

"I'll have to thank him later. Gosh, I still can't believe he set all of this up."

"Yeah, I couldn't either. I figured you guys must have made amends. That boy sincerely cares for you," she says. I fill her in quickly about Ivy and Melissa even though he told me he didn't have sex with her. "Regardless of his bed partners, you still have his heart Lourdes. I can tell that just from my conversations with him during our planning to get me here.

Not saying that you two need to be together or that he's going to change his manwhoring. I'm just saying, at the root of it all, he's definitely still in love with you. Denial is a powerful thing." She winks.

"You found time to talk to him. Why didn't you return my messages?" I ask, pinching her.

"Ouch!" she shrieks, rubbing her arm before laughing. "Okay, I deserved that."

"Damn straight. That and then some," I laugh with her.

"To be honest, I was busy with the start of classes and trying not to miss my best friend. When Diesel reached out to me, I knew if I talked with you, I would let it slip. You know how hard it is for me to keep shit from you and that's just regular shit. This was huge and I didn't want to ruin it."

"I had to hold a lot of crap in. I had nobody to rant to. I finally shared my feelings with Lily today so it was nice to get it all out with someone I can trust." Brooke gives me a fake frown. "Stop it. You're still my bestie. You just weren't around when I needed to unload all this emotional turmoil. I feel like I was on a damn rollercoaster that I couldn't get off of."

"It's barely been two weeks," she argues.

"Yup. Plenty of time for shit to hit the fan. Did you know that Sevyn is here?"

"Shut the fuck up? Really? Why?" She pulls me down on the bed. Apparently, she didn't get my message about that. "Oh my God. You have been dealing with a lot if he's here. I'm sorry I wasn't there for you and I'm glad you had Lily to talk to." My goal wasn't to make her feel bad.

"It's okay, Brooke. He had some business he needed to work through with Diesel from what I can gather. They sat

CREED of Redemption

me down and explained the reasoning for what they did and we're okay now."

"What was it? Why did they switch in and out at the lake house? Because for the life of me, I can't understand why he would need to keep the fact that he had a twin from you."

"I can't tell you that. Diesel shared some things with me in confidence that I can't share. Just know the reasoning was legitimate, and I forgave them."

"Well, that's all I need to know. Then I forgive them too. Diesel had already somewhat redeemed himself with me when he showed how intent he was on getting me here to be with you for a weekend." She wipes away the new tears that have leaked from my eyes. "None of that. Let's get you ready so I can meet some of the celebrity hunks."

"What about Michael?" Is she already done with him?

"Meh. He's moving too slow. He hasn't made me his, so I'm free to do whatever I please." She smiles. Michael is an idiot. Brooke doesn't give options for more. She's not a womanwhore because she doesn't sleep with all of the men she dates. She's just very picky and it's hard for them to keep her interest. She gets bored easily. So if she was willing to have more with Michael, it means she really liked him. Guys can be so dense sometimes.

"His loss," I say shaking my head. "He better hope that one of these celebrity guys don't snatch you up this weekend."

"Yup. Now let me do your hair. You know I love that fucking dress on you. This is the perfect time for her to make her debut," she says about the dress. "I know exactly the hairstyle for this." Brooke does my makeup first. Lily comes out and asks for hers to be done next. Brooke agrees, but she

141

first does her magic on me. After she finishes my makeup, she puts my hair in a low chignon. I almost don't recognize myself. I look and feel beautiful. I'm ready for the party now. It's amazing the confidence you can get from looking the best you've ever looked and having your best friend by your side.

Now nightfall, we finally head into the house where the party is in full swing. It's mostly contained out back and under the covered lanai. Rock music seems to come from every direction and the wait staff walking around with drinks are plentiful. There are also a few open bars scattered around the perimeter. We lose Lily almost instantly because she ditches our asses to find her man. I swear those two can't be separated from each other for any considerable amount of time. It's just Brooke and I until the drummer from Reckless Ambition asks her to have a drink with him at the bar. I think his name is Jack. She looks over at me, unsure because she doesn't want to leave me alone. She's not my babysitter so I tell her to go and that we will meet up later. She hesitantly leaves with Jack. I grab a drink from the next waiter guy that passes. I have no idea what the hell it is, but it's brown and nasty as shit. I gulp it down anyway because whatever it is, it's strong and I need my buzz back. Now that I'm standing alone, I'm not so confident.

I consider going to the bar and just people watching, but strong arms wrap around my waist from behind.

"Hmmm, wearing red again I see." I don't have to look over my shoulder to know it's Diesel. "Did you wear this for me, Lourdes?" I look around nervously because we are out in the open. People can see us. I try to pull away, but he pulls me closer into him.

"Someone will see us," I comment nervously.

"Maybe," he agrees. "Come with me then," he urges. I can smell the heady scent of whiskey.

"What if I don't want to?" I challenge. He rubs his hardened cock against my ass and I squeeze my legs together. *There goes those damn vagina butterflies again.* Logically, I know what will happen if I follow him, yet in this moment, I ache for him. I ache for the inevitable.

"Your choice, princess. We can stay right here and let the whole party watch me," he says twirling a lock of hair that has escaped my chignon.

"Watch you do what?" I ask breathily. The way he calls me princess is so damn hot. He hasn't called me that in a while and I realize I've missed it. My skin is heated and wetness coats my panties, just from his proximity and thinking about what he wants to do to me—just from him calling me princess.

"Do you really want to find out?" I turn my head slightly to look at him and shake my head no. He winks at me. That wink has to be the sexiest thing ever. He's toying with me again and I'm letting him. "Thought so. Follow me, babe."

He lets me go and walks in the opposite direction into the house. I wait a few seconds before I follow his lead, careful not to be obvious. From this view I can admire how fucking hot he is without fear of being caught staring. He wears his jeans well. Nice muscular legs and the perfect ass. His band t-shirt is so simple, yet the package that is not so hidden through the fabric makes you want to trace every line of defined goodness. His body truly is a work of perfection.

While following him up the winding staircase and into

one of the bedroom suites, I already know that I will be giving in to my desires. Tomorrow he will go back to being off limits, but tonight I want him. My thoughts are interrupted by the slam of the door and my back being pushed against it.

"So, princess, you purposefully ignored my little warning earlier about seeing you in red." He raises both of my arms above my head and secures them with one hand. "This fucking dress is so damn sinful—a tease to my cock. I couldn't even focus on the party. The moment I saw you, I knew you had worn it for me. Admit it." He runs a finger through the keyhole of my dress.

"Diesel…yes," I admit.

"Yes what?" he pushes.

"Yes sir," I correct. He growls and the mood in the room changes.

"That is not what I meant, Lourdes," he says. That fucking delicious rasp of his is back. I know the tone well. I recognize what it means. His alter ego—the Dom—has been turned on. It's a shame that he suppresses this side of himself, but I'm seeing it now. He let's go of my hands, seemingly unsure of how to proceed. He runs a hand through his hair. I've never done this before so I don't know what the hell I'm doing or if it's even a real thing, but I have to try. If this is the only night I will allow myself to have him, I want all of him. I want the side that he hides from everybody else.

I slowly take off my heels and put them to the side. Next I undress until only my panties are left. He watches me with rapt attention—waiting to see what I will do next. His heart is beating wildly against my chest and my nerves are threatening to unleash the alcohol I drank. Still I push forward. Tonight I give him all of me in exchange for all of him. Careful not to look him in the eyes, I drop to my knees and then sit back on my heels. I bow my head and hope that he accepts my submission.

"Holy fuck me," he swears. "Lourdes, what are you doing?" he asks in disbelief. His rasp of authority is overshadowed with concern. The high pitch of his voice right now is not right. With my eyes closed and head still bowed, I can't see his reaction, but I can sense him slipping away from giving me what I want. I allow my mind to wander to the first time he shared his real self with me. I distinctly remember the tone of his voice, the strength of his touch, and how special he made me feel that he was sharing a side of himself with me that he didn't show other people.

"Lourdes?" He addresses me again, but I remain mute. I allow myself to slip further and further into that memory. "God damn, Lourdes, answer me." A euphoric feeling moves through my body, and I feel like I'm floating. Then I hear it. He's back.

"Lourdes! Look at me now!"

I lift my head until my eyes find his. Light filters through the curtains from the moon, but I don't miss the intensity in his stare.

"Yes, sir," I finally say.

He levels his gaze on me. "Remember you asked for this," he warns. "You better be fucking ready," he growls.

"Sir. Yes sir," I repeat. I hear the ominous sound of the door locking. He walks away from me to turn on a lamp by the bed. There is already whiskey there so he had to have been in here prior. I watch as he pours himself a drink and takes a few hefty swallows before pulling his shirt over his head. I'm still half naked, on my knees in the center of the room. I won't move from this spot until he tells me to though. My eyes narrow as he removes his shoes and socks. Jeans and bare fucking feet again. Sweet Jesus.

"Get over here." Those three words are music to my ears. "Stop," he commands when I'm a little more than an arm's length away from him. "Move your arms and let me see your beautiful fucking tits."

"I…" The words die on my lips. His eyebrows arch in question. He doesn't want to hear my excuses or deal with my insecurities. I was much bolder when all the lights were off. I hadn't even realized that I had subconsciously crossed my arms to hide my breasts. I slowly lower my arms and hear him inhale a sharp breath. I stare at the floor as a feelings of vulnerability cross over me.

"Look at me, Lourdes," he commands. I look at him and watch as he sits on the bed and leans back against the head-board. "You wanted to play, so play we shall. You've awakened my demons, so tonight I'll let you get reacquainted with them," he promises.

"Yes, sir," I say simply. I don't trust myself to say much more than that. I'm excited and nervous at the same time. If this is our last time together like this, I don't want him holding anything back.

"This is your last chance to grab that fucking dick tease you call a dress and run as far as you can Lourdes," he warns a little to calmly. "You're about to unleash something you better be ready for because I have no plans of letting you leave this room without a thorough look at the shit I'm into." The ache that intensifies between my legs answers for me. I want it all. I want him to show me.

"I'm not running, sir," I insist. "Show me." His wicked smile ensures me that I've sealed my fate. He pulls a remote of some kind from the nightstand next to the bed. With the push of a few buttons, The Weekend's *Wicked Games* filters through the speakers around the room. A few notes and lyrics pass with us just staring at each other.

"Strip for me," he commands. I begin to take off my panties, but he stops me. "No. Strip for me as in perform for me. Show me how much you want my cock." I swallow the lump in my throat. If this is my test, I don't plan to fail.

CHAPTER
Fifteen

DIESEL

I TRIED TO NOT WANT HER. I MEAN I REALLY FUCKING TRIED. Then today at the pool, my dick decided not to listen. Although she has a body made for sin, there's more to it than that. It's everything about her—her fucking existence. The more I try to deny my need to have her, the more she consumes my every thought. I couldn't even accept the advances Melissa was throwing my way because it wouldn't have been fair to her. I couldn't lead her on. I was so sure that I would find a piece of ass tonight, to fuck my desire for her from my system, until I laid eyes on her. I couldn't help myself. She had the only pussy I was interested in tonight so here we are. I didn't expect her to submit. I didn't fucking expect her to awaken the part of me that I try so hard to suppress. She's only gotten a small taste of the fucked-up shit I'm into, but tonight I will not hold back.

I only worry that she doesn't fully comprehend what she's awakened, but she will. She will experience all facets of me tonight. Maybe after she runs from the sick shit I enjoy, I can finally move on. First, I will break down her inhibitions. Once those walls come down, I will show her what's on the other side. I tell her to strip and watch as she struggles with the task. Her natural instinct is to hide herself, yet she wants to please me.

The music is slow and climactic. The lyrics are so fitting for this moment, for this dance I have her giving me. She slowly lowers her panties down her legs and then removes them one leg at a time. Her clean shaven pussy makes my cock jump. She turns her back to me as she lets her hips sway to the music. I suspect not having to look at me gives her the confidence she needs to keep dancing. That's okay for now since I'm enjoying the view. The round curve of her ass has me wanting to end her little performance right now and just bury my dick deep inside her pussy.

"Turn around," I tell her after I've had enough of just seeing the back of her. I need to look in her eyes because my dick is urging me to move this along. I refill my glass with Jameson, but's it's not for me. I take the glass and join her where she stands. "Open." I rub the glass along the seam of her lips and she opens her mouth for me. Her face frowns on the first sip, but improves with each subsequent sip of the whiskey. Her features relax and her eyelids become hooded. I take the last of it remaining in the glass into my mouth, but then I find her lips and make her open for me again. Our tongues dance as the liquor is transferred from my mouth to hers. It burns so good while I try to consume the taste of her.

"*Hmmm*," she purrs. Her hooded lids lower even further when I trail kisses from her neck to her pebbled nipples. I think she's ready. I let my hand travel south until my fingers are slipping through her wetness.

She moves against my fingers, but I remove them. When she comes for the first time tonight, it will be on my dick and not my fingers. I lift her slowly and watch her eyes widen with surprise when she finds herself over my head—her dripping pussy in my direct line of vision. I put her legs over my shoulders and walk her to the nearest wall. When I'm sure she can't squirm too much, I bury my face between her legs. Her essence smells so damn sweet. I should have at least unzipped my jeans to give my dick room to throb. Too late now. My first tentative lick has her throwing her head back against the wall.

"Hold on, baby." I twirl my tongue around her clit, teasing it, worshipping it. Lourdes wriggles in my arms, trying to get away from my cunnilingus. I get a tighter grip on her ass and push my face deeper. I suck on her clit with even more determination and watch as her eyes begin to roll back.

"Die...sel," she mumbles incoherently. The trembling of her legs around my neck confirms that she is oh so close. I'm not ready to let her cum though so I slide my tongue through to her entrance. I slap her ass, enough to sting, but not enough to cause pain. I'm diverting her focus because I don't want her cumming yet. Soon she will realize my true kink—orgasm denial. I thrust my tongue in and out of her soaking wet pussy until she is riding my face.

"That's it, baby. Ride my fucking face. Make that sweet pussy take all of my tongue." She grinds harder and I almost want to let her have the release that she is craving right now… almost. I lift her over my head once more to switch her the opposite direction—her ass lines up with my face as her legs work to get situated behind my neck. She is facing away from me in this position. Her legs instantly wrap around my head and neck when I begin to lower her body down mine. A small gasp of air comes out in a rush from her when I let her drop to the level I need her. I secure my arms around the base of her ass once her face is in the vicinity with my dick. "Undo me, Lourdes."

She palms my dick through my jeans before she finally frees my cock. It juts to attention, ready to be sucked. My tongue licks a path between her opening and her ass. She tightens up, but I smile because I will be taking her here again tonight. For now though, I have lined us up for a little sixty-nine. She seizes the opportunity to be the first to initiate. Without being told, she grabs my cock and takes me to the back of her throat. Seeing her suck my dick upside down, gives me pause.

"*Hmmm*," she hums around my dick and the sensation is un-fucking-believable. I thrust my hardened length into her mouth and time it with the thrusts of my tongue inside her pussy. My nose is buried between her ass cheeks as I work to go deeper with every thrust. The smell of her, combined with the slow attention she is giving my cock, has my legs stiffening. I feel myself getting close. She plays with my balls while licking the vein that runs underneath the head of my dick. It jumps with each pass of her tongue. She goes back to sucking me, taking me deeper each time until she has my entire dick in her mouth. Holy shit. I can feel the tingle begin to creep up my balls in this position.

I need her to slow down, it's getting increasingly hard not to explode in her mouth. I slap her ass once more and she's startled for a second. A second is all I need. Once her mouth is away from my cock, I flip her once more. This time her legs are around my waist. I allow her to slide down my body until that wet pussy of hers is sitting just above my cock. No priming needed. I slam into her and I have to hold on to her tightly. She arches her back and instantly begins to ride my dick. All shyness forgotten. I don't move at first. I let her set the rhythm—do what feels good to her. I slowly join the pace she has set for us. The sound of her soaking pussy echoes over the music that is playing as my balls slap her ass.

Lourdes

I'm so lost in Diesel right now. My pussy feels so full as I grip his every thrust. I need him deeper still, only the grip he has on my hips is restricting my movements. He is only giving me the amount of dick he wants me to have.

"Please go deeper, Diesel," I beg and he arches an eyebrow at me. He angles his hips and slams into me a few times and my pussy becomes an inferno. He slows his pace, but I need hard, deep, and fast.

"Can't come yet, baby," he teases as he slides his dick out of me. My pussy immediately clenches at its disappearance.

Diesel stands me back on my feet and my legs feel weak. Holy hell this man is strong. His lifts and the flips have my head swimming. I need a second to adjust to the position change. I didn't even know he had that in his bag of tricks. It's hot as hell.

"Get out of your head and get your sexy ass on the bed, Lourdes," he commands. I wobble over to the bed and crawl onto it. "I like that view. Stay just like that." I'm on all fours for him. He walks up behind me and slaps each ass cheek again. The delicious sting has my pussy dripping with need. I clench my pussy once more to dull the ache, but it only intensifies. "So fucking wet," he says.

"Fuck me, Diesel. I need your thick cock to fill me—to make me come."

"In time, princess," he teases as he kneels down to lick me from behind again. The feeling is fucking amazing, but then he stops. His teasing has me so wound up, I feel like I'm about to explode from his deprival. He builds me up over and over again, forbidding me from having my release. I don't know how much more I can take. "Head down and ass up, baby, so that pussy opens up for me." Fuck, I love his dirty talk. He can have anything he wants if he will just let me come.

I do as he instructs and he inserts a few fingers. He massages my insides before replacing his fingers with the tip of his beautiful cock. I throb around him. I back my ass up to him until his cock is resting at the hilt. He restricts me from moving farther, so I can feel his girth. I put a greater arch in my back to entice him to move. I need him to come undone. He wraps my hair in his fist and pulls at the same time he slams into me.

I meet him stroke for stroke, my legs beginning to feel weak as my orgasm nears. When he pulls out of me, once again before I can get my release, my body collapses in defeat. He flips me over onto my back, but I just lay there. I can no longer move. Tears stream down my face in frustration and the room blurs into a haze.

"There it is. True submission," Diesel smirks. His voice sounds like we're underwater. He wipes my tears away. "No tears, baby. Now I'm going to give you what you've been wanting all night."

He pushes my legs over his shoulders and eases into me. In this position, his cock is almost too much. He starts slowly, but then he finally comes undone. He fucks me hard and fast. He deepens his strokes, but I'm numb.

"Fuccccckkkkk, baby," he screams as he pulls out and comes all over my stomach. I close my eyes because the out-of-body experience is a foreign one. I feel so out of control, but he seems to get off on seeing me like this. I didn't even cum. What the hell is going on with me?

He jumps out of the bed and comes back with a damp towel. He begins to clean me up and I just continue to lay here—embarrassed that I just zoned the fuck out.

"Diesel, I—" I begin, but he shushes me with a single finger to my lips.

"Enough for tonight, baby. Let me just hold you." He slides in bed next to me and pulls me into his arms. He kisses the top of my head and actually rocks me.

The motion is soothing. The foggy haze begins to dissipate and I snuggle closer into his arms.

"Sleep now, Lourdes," he says. His rocking slows, and I know that he is out. I replay the night back. He stated that was enough for tonight which means he didn't give me his all. He's still holding something back. I don't get it. I don't understand what made me cry, or why it got him off, for that matter. His tender care for me afterwards proves he doesn't want to see me hurt so why was it that he could only cum after seeing my tears. I'm so confused. I don't know how to feel about tonight. I wanted all of him, the part of himself that he doesn't show to anyone else, so I'll try to understand.

I'm more embarrassed about my own actions. I had this beautiful man on top of me, fucking me like a sex god and I just laid here motionless and numb. Honestly I don't see how he could have gotten off. I totally checked out and it was beyond my control. It was like I was here, but I wasn't. He might as well have been screwing a corpse. That has never happened to me before. I went from insatiable to frigid. He just got his nut and then called it quits. He probably thinks I can't handle the shit he's into and from my reaction tonight, I'd say he's right. I asked for this. I need to be by myself right now.

I ease his arm from around me until I'm completely out from under him. I try to remember where I first removed my clothes. I crawl around on the floor until I finally find them. Diesel turns over in the bed, but thankfully stays asleep. I throw my dress back on, foregoing the heels. I can't find the panties so screw it. I tiptoe out of the door, with my stilettos in hand, careful not to wake him.

The music is still going strong out back, but no way am

I returning to the party. I find the bedroom that Lily and I changed into our swimsuits in earlier. Luckily the room is empty. I was afraid all of the bedrooms would be taken by now. I can't decide if I should put the lock on the door or not. Brooke and Lily may need to come in here to sleep later. On the other hand, I don't want someone stumbling in here after I'm asleep, looking for a place to have sex. Mind made up, I put the lock on the door. I'm glad I had the idea to bring up something to sleep in. I change into my sleep shorts and tank, then crawl into this bed fit for a queen, with its million thread count sheets.

My phone buzzes on the charger next to the bed. I think it may have been Diesel waking up to find me gone, but it's text messages from Brooke. I didn't have my phone on me and I only pulled it out of my bag when I changed into my sleep clothes.

There are like ten missed calls and even more messages. All asking where the hell I am. I reply back to her text since I'm not in the mood to explain shit that I'm not sure of myself.

Me: Sorry just saw your missed calls and texts. My phone was upstairs in my bag. I hope my message will suffice and she can go back to partying with Jack, if she even gets this right now. *No such luck.*

Brooke: I was worried that you may have been drunk off your ass somewhere with some douche trying to get in your pants. Where are you?

Me: I'm fine Brooke. I'm calling it a night. I'm in the bedroom that is the first to the right. I locked the door so I wouldn't be disturbed by people looking to find a hook up spot. I can unlock it if you're coming up.

Brooke: I'm glad you're okay. Keep your phone close. If things don't work out with Jack, I'll be joining you tonight. Let's wish me luck though. I accidentally felt it and he's pierced.

Me: Good luck with that. That's Brooke. She sees something she wants, she just goes after it. Michael is a fool for not snatching her up. Most don't even get that option.

Brooke: Thanks Chica. Talk to you in the morning— hopefully.

I leave the phone next to my pillow in case Lily or Brooke call to get in the room but I highly doubt it. Xander is not going to let Lily out of his sight, especially if he has an opportunity to get some real alone time with her. Plus Jack would have to be a dumbass to turn down Brooke, so it looks like I'll have this wonderful bed all to myself. I'll ponder the Diesel thing tomorrow, but tonight I just want to sleep.

CHAPTER
Sixteen

DIESEL

I'T'S TIME TO GET READY FOR REHEARSAL THIS MORNING, but I don't even want to leave this room. What the fuck was I thinking last night? The worst fucking demon I possess showed itself last night. Lourdes never stood a chance. She started us down that path of me unleashing my kink, but I should have stopped it. I look around this room now and instead of reminiscing about how good it felt to have her again, I'm ashamed. I fucked up. I didn't properly assess her readiness for the shit that gets me off. I let my own lust cloud my judgment. Orgasm denial is one thing, but my desire to completely break someone through this denial is just plain evil.

Experienced submissives will normally enter psychological subspace when denied their orgasm for an extended amount of time. The pleasure is so intense, their mind shuts down and the body surrenders to the total will of the Dom. The decision to submit comes from the body and not the mind in this instance. It is the ultimate form of submission and a sign of complete control. It can't be faked. After I've reached this pentacle of control from my submissive's body, I can then allow myself to cum. The submissive is rewarded with multiple orgasms—only this didn't come to pass with Lourdes. I was caught off guard by her tears last night and I reacted terribly. I came so fucking hard because those tears were like a gift. A twisted, fucked-up gift. It was her surrendering to me in a way that nobody ever has before. Her intense need for me was overwhelming. I fucked her so hard to give her what she desperately needed. I wanted to feel her cum around my cock and she didn't.

It was then, the magnitude of my actions hit me. The woman lying there with me was lost in subspace and completely broken. I've never been riddled with so much guilt like this. And now to wake up and find out she's not still here by my side, scares the shit out of me. Did I go too far? I know I need to go find her. This may have just set us several steps backwards. I need to fix this.

The house is really quiet so I'm guessing the guys are still in their rooms hungover. I'm glad I kept my drinking to a minimal last night. I search for Lourdes and I finally find her in the library of all places. Her back is to me as she admires some books in front of her. She pulls one from the shelf and when she spins around, I'm there in her personal space. She drops the book in surprise. I bend down to pick the book up for her and I can tell she doesn't know where to look. She looks all round, anywhere but at me. I place the book back on the shelf and grab her hand. The awkwardness between us is palpable, but I have to try to normalize things again.

"I'm sorry, Lourdes," I say for the first time.

"I don't know why I had the meltdown. Yes, you teased the hell out of me and made me want you so freaking bad, but I can't explain what came over me." She sniffles. She looks away, trying not to cry. She turns her back to me—I hate when she does this. The fact that she can't face me. "God the fucking tears won't stop. I'm the one who is sorry. I practically begged to have all of you and then I completely freaked the hell out."

"Fuck." I cringe. She's still in an emotional state and doesn't even have an understanding of why. "Come here, baby." I wrap my arms around her from behind and just hold her.

"Sorry, Diesel, I—,"

"Don't you dare. You did nothing wrong. I fucked up. I brought you to subspace, not thinking about how it would affect someone who has never experienced it. I will make this up to you. Just please tell me you will let me. Please tell me that my fucked-up desires haven't pushed you away—" She spins around in my arms and brings my lips down to hers. She kisses me slowly and this feels different. I lift her so that her legs wrap around my waist. She's wearing those shorts again so my hands gladly palm her ass to keep her from slipping. Our tongues meet and I'm lost in her. I don't want to let her lips go. I want them bruised from my passion and my need for her. I can feel the tables starting to turn and I'm powerless to stop it. I suck on her neck and her little intake of breath makes me hard. I won't go there with her now, but I sure as hell want to. I want to give her the orgasms she deserves.

"Well, I didn't fucking see this coming," we hear from behind us. It's Gable. *Shit.* "Xander is going to kick your ass, Diesel. What the fuck, man?" I have no explanations for him right now. There is nothing I can say or make up. We're busted. I let Lourdes down and then whisper to her that it will be okay.

"I'm going to go," she whispers back. "Talk later."

"Don't say anything, Gable," she pleads on her way out. He nods at her but doesn't give her an answer either way. She closes the library door that I fucking left open. No wonder I didn't hear anyone come in. Not that I would have with Lourdes as my distraction, but still.

"Of all the pussy you have access to now, you choose our band member's sister?" he fumes. "You know how Xander feels about her, man. This could ruin everything. Why her? Why take the risk?"

"First off, watch your fucking mouth. Don't ever compare Lourdes to the groupie bitches ever again." Now I'm the one fuming.

"Shiiiittt. It's worse than I thought. How long has this been going on? Are you two a thing?"

"I don't know what we are," I admit. I purposely ignore the *how-long* question. Truth is, I don't have a clue. I know I don't want a relationship again, but I want her. Not as a fucking friend either. I want her in my bunk—free to do whatever the hell we want without hiding it. I know I can't have that with her though, and it fuels my anger. "Look, just keep what you saw quiet and shit will be okay."

"Whatever, man. This is going to blow up in all of our faces. You want her because you're not supposed to have her," he huffs and storms out.

Could he be right? I have this insane attachment to her, but what if it's another symptom of my need for control. She's supposed to be off limits and I say fuck the limits.

The more somebody tells me no, the more I rebel. It's a scary possibility that what Gable just concluded is indeed my reality. Knowing this doesn't change the way I feel. I want her. We will not have a repeat of last night, but she will be underneath me again.

I head to meet the guys at rehearsal. They look like shit, but we're doing this. Gable is already here and doesn't make eye contact. Fine by me. What I do with my dick is none of his business.

"Keyser and Xander, set us up with the rifts from Ben Khan's *Drive*," I suggest. They nod and give me the distraction I need. Gable joins us on drums and the rehearsal begins. I love the sexiness of this song. The sensual lyrics against the melody are definitely a panty dropper. *"Let's have sex in the back seat,"* I sing.

Reckless Ambition walks in just as we begin and Anderson immediately takes his place next to me after grabbing one of the mics. He begins to sing an octave below me and the shit just works.

"Fuck yeah!" Ivy yells, looking to find another mic. Xander nods in the direction of one sitting on the piano we're not using. She grabs it and winks at me. I guess she's not too upset with me anymore. "*Let's have sex in the back seat*," she joins in a couple octaves above us. We look between each other with grins on our faces because we know we have straight fire with this one. Even Gable is smiling now.

We find another song for Ivy and I to do a duet to before we wrap it up. Tonight is going to be epic. Now to fix things with Gable. No need for shit between us to be weird. I get his concern. Taking the high road can be pretty damn exhausting, but I need our band focused on our music and not on my sex life.

Lourdes

"Where did you disappear to last night?" Lily inquires. We're backstage watching our guys perform from the monitors in their dressing room.

"I was around," I answer nonchalantly,

"You hear that Brooke? She was around," Lily giggles.

"I heard," Brooke says joining the laughter.

"Funny thing is. I guess Diesel was *around* too. I overheard the guys looking for him a couple times to do some shots. They assumed he was with Ivy, but I happen to know she was upstairs hooking up with the lead singer, Jude, from Insanity."

"That little slut. I guess she likes her lead singers," I joke. This news makes me immensely happy. Let her move on to someone else.

"Uh-uh." Lily shakes her finger. "Don't try to change the subject. Did you have your own hook up session going on with a lead singer?" I try to turn away from her because I don't want her to see my guilty expression, but I'm too slow. "You little bitch," she laughs.

"Hush it. Brooke went off with that Jack dude and you were with Xander. I was a sitting duck," I explain.

"And what? You ran into Diesel and your legs fell open?" Lily teases. Brooke cracks the hell up.

"That's the real reason you didn't return my texts until later, isn't it? He wore you out and then you needed to go to bed early," Brooke jokes. If she only knew how accurate she was.

"You two are terrible." I roll my eyes. "I've already said too much." I'm not going to give them a play by play. Their vanilla minds couldn't handle it anyway. I wonder how one would classify my mind since it's no longer vanilla yet I'm not all that experienced either?

"We already know you were with Diesel," Brooke says. "I hope you know what you're doing. The mouth always says one thing and the body does another. Be careful and don't let your guard down. If you're just getting a little of that yummi-ness for yourself, I say good for you."

I give her the thumbs up. "I agree," Lily says. "Now that the mystery of where you were is figured out, let's fix our-selves a drink."

"One drink," I agree. I don't need a repeat of their last show where I needed a babysitter and had Xander pissed at me. I pour myself some Jameson from the guys' stash and

I'm hit with memories from last night. A tingle hits me between the legs, remembering drinking from his mouth. I'm watching him perform with Anderson and Ivy but he has my complete attention. He's singing about having sex in the back seat and all I can think about is wanting that with him. My pussy picks now to get her act together—when I'm not actually getting the dick.

I see Ivy put her slutty hands on his chest as she sings the lyrics with him and I swear my heart skips a few beats. Diesel backs away to keep from being obvious in his diss. He smiles at her but then goes to the front of the stage and seduces the women in the crowd. He lifts his tank to show off that fucking washboard of his and they go nuts. His reaction to Ivy was subtle, but not so much to us. Brooke and Lily turn to look at me and we smile because he didn't give into her advances. She needs to just stick with that Jude guy and leave Diesel alone. I finish my Jameson straight and watch the rest of their performance on a high. He is going to get so much pussy for that move. I'll see to it.

Tonight is our last night at the mansion. We're heading to Texas in the morning where they have three tour stops. Brooke leaves in the morning, but I'm craving Diesel. I need to make up for last night. We're sitting around the bedroom talking about her hook up with Jack last night, and his piercing, but my mind keeps wondering where Diesel is. I know Reckless Ambition is still here too. What if she got her hooks in him now.

"Call him, Lourdes," Brooke says suddenly.

"What? No. We need to enjoy your last night here before you have to go back."

"Look, I can see your mind is preoccupied and I can't say that I blame you," she smiles. "You know once you two are back on the bus, there will be no chance for sex, so get it now. I'll cover for you if anyone asks."

"Are you sure? I mean, I can come right back. I just need to see him," I explain.

"Yeah. See him inside you." She's in hysterics now.

"Very funny." I shove her and she laughs harder. "I'll be back. Nobody should be looking for me. I know Keyser and Gable have their own hook ps. Xander is somewhere up Lily's ass."

"Probably literally," Brooke says laughing at what I just unknowingly insinuated. "Now go so you can get back and tell me all about it." I roll my eyes, but let her push me out the door.

I walk out into the hall just in time to see Ivy knocking on Diesel's door—the same room he had me in last night. He opens the door only half way, but I can't make out what they're saying. He finally looks past her and sees me. I don't want to see if he lets her in but I don't want to retreat back to the room with Brooke either. I can't face the questions that will surely come from her about why I'm back so soon. I head downstairs with no plan in mind. I finally decide to head to the library again, sure nobody will be in there. I'll wait about an hour and go back to the room with Brooke. My mind is running a mile a minute. Why isn't she still upset with him after the whole Melissa showdown? Did he make it up to her somehow? Did he only sidestep her advances on stage because he knew I was watching? God, I'm so stupid. I bet she won't freeze up and zone out like I did last night. I bet a woman like her knows how to handle him.

I pace from one end of the room to the other. I look up when I hear the door shut and the distinct click of it being locked. "So where were we before we were interrupted earlier?" Diesel asks, standing by the door.

"Don't you have Ivy waiting on you?" I sass. He closes the distance and has me pinned against the bookshelf so quickly, I barely have time to react.

"Does it look like I care? You're the one I came to find!" He secures my arms above my head with one hand while his tatted arm slides under my shirt and underneath my bra. He massages my tits and just like that all my anger just leaves my body. I close my eyes, but they snap open when he nips at my lips. "Keep them open," he commands. He removes both of his hands, but somehow, I just know to keep my arms above my head. He digs in his pockets for something and I think he's searching for a condom. I know we didn't use one last night. Bad idea, but I know he's usually diligent about wrapping it up. I still remember the freak out he had when we first slipped up. I hope that it's only me that he can be free with because I need him in me now. The hotness raging in my jeans means I'm ready tonight.

"I need to come, Diesel," I say brazenly.

"And come you shall, Lourdes. That I can promise." He smirks.

CHAPTER
Seventeen

Lourdes

WHEN DIESEL PULLS MY BLACK LACE PANTIES FROM his pocket, my jaw drops in shock. I guess he found them in the room. He sniffs them and something about the act makes me wetter for him. He runs them along my cheek as he instructs me to open my mouth. When I do, he puts my fucking panties in mouth. Holy shit! The ache is unbearable now. This is so dirty, yet so damn hot at the same time. I keep my arms above my head and watch as he slides his belt from his pants. He loops it around my wrists and then tightens until my wrists are securely bound.

"Three rules baby," he says. I nod my understanding so he continues. "No touching. No looking away. No screaming,

Lourdes. I nod again and watch as he undoes the button of his jeans. I try not to melt against this fucking shelf when he makes a show of getting naked for me. His body is so damn beautiful. His thick, pink erection is its own masterpiece. It should be framed in a gallery somewhere as evidence a cock can be this gorgeous. I can't even look at it without wanting it in my mouth. "See something you want, Lourdes?" he asks, noticing all my focus on his dick.

I can only nod since he has me gagged. I could spit out the panties, but where is the fun in that?

"*Hmmm*. I bet." His eyes darken with mischief and I know shit is about to get real. He pulls down my jeans and panties in one pull.

He removes my shoes so I can step out of them. He then flips my shirt over my head and lets it rest behind my neck, further constricting my arms. He unhooks my bra from the front and lets it fall open to him. My whole body is one big, sensitive ball of need. He kisses my neck and massages my tits with both hands. I'm trying not to close my eyes like he instructed because I know he wants me to watch, but it's hard. When his tongue twirls around my nipples, I can't help the moan that escapes around my panties. He just smiles up at me as he continues his path south.

"You have the sweetest pussy, baby. My dick has been hard for this all day," Diesel tells me. He drops to his hands and knees in front of me and wraps one of my legs around his shoulders. With the first lick to my clit, my eyes close of their own accord and he stops. My eyes snap open and he rewards me by continuing. He sucks on my clit and every nerve comes alive. He slides a couple of fingers in me and begins to finger fuck me. I'm riding his hand and I can feel my orgasm already building. He sucks harder and it takes everything in me not to fucking scream. His finger makes a come here motion and I squirt everywhere. The waves won't stop. He puts my leg down mid orgasm and turns me around. He positions my arms to rest on the Queen Anne chair next to us. He uses some of my wetness to coat my ass before telling me to push out.

We've done this before, so I know what he wants me to do. He slides his dick into my ass slowly and begins to massage my clit. My orgasm rolls right into another one as I push back further onto him. He surprises me by pulling the panties from my mouth.

"Whose ass is this, Lourdes?"

"Yours," I answer without hesitation between moans. His pace picks up and his balls slap against my pussy. Anyone that happens to pass could hear the punishing fuck he's giving me and it makes me that much wetter for some reason.

He drives deeper in me and I want him deeper still. I can't get enough.

"Shit I'm going to come, baby. Where do you want it?" he asks through shaky breaths.

"My ass," I reply. Crazy how he can fuck the shyness right out of me.

"In or on," he seeks to clarify. "Tell me, baby. I can't hold on anymore."

"Wherever you want, baby," I assure, echoing his term of endearment. He slams into me now as he races toward his own release. Seeing him come undone is enough to send me over the edge with him. He continues his assault on my clit while he comes, making sure to milk every bit from me. He comes inside my ass, his choice of where being made clear. I'm so spent that my legs threaten to buckle underneath me. He undoes the belt and rubs my wrists.

I sink down to the floor and he follows me down. "That was hot," I say after I finally catch my breath. I remove my shirt and bra the rest of the way.

"Agreed," he says rolling over onto his back. "Now get that sexy ass up here. I'm not done with you yet. Far from it." His engorged cock lengthens along his stomach and my greedy pussy pulsates from the sight. I straddle his thighs, finding my second wind. I lift up slightly so he put his dick where it needs to be before I ease down his length. "So damn wet," he comments.

I start to move. I start slow, indulging in the feel of his thickness filling me to capacity. But then his hands grab my hips and I know my perceived control is being snatched right out from under me. He slams me down on his cock in time with the thrust of his own hips. He bounces me on his dick until our rhythm is one.

"Your dick feels so good inside me. I can feel you so deep, Diesel," I cry out. I take us faster as I feel the telltale sign of my orgasm. I've lost count of how many he has given me tonight.

His finger enters my ass, and he slams into me even harder.

"How deep do you feel me now Lourdes? Now that I'm filling you from both ends?"

"*Unnnnnnnnn,*" I moan. I can't form a coherent thought, let alone actual words.

"Those fucking tits are fucking amazing to watch while you take my dick in your slick pussy and my finger in your ass. Your skin is flushed and I can tell you're about to explode all over my dick. The clench of your pussy tells me you're so close baby." His fucking dirty talk undoes me. I explode all over his cock just like he predicted. He brings my grinding hips to a halt so I can feel his throbbing deep within my walls. We stare deeply into each other's eyes as our orgasms intertwine in one epic fucking release. Something passes between us. I can't put my finger on it, but I can feel the change.

He slaps my ass and gives me the sexiest grin ever. "Now to get you back to your friend, babe. I know you want to spend a little time with Brooke before she leaves," he suggests.

"What about you? Are you going back to your friend to?" I tease, referencing Ivy.

"Not a chance," he assures. "Now get your sexy ass dressed before I hold you hostage here as my sex slave."

I hope he doesn't think that's supposed to be a deterrent. That just makes me want to stay. "So convincing," I remark.

He gets up first and hands me my clothes. "Get going, sex fiend. Gah, I may have created a monster." I take my clothes from him and begin to get dressed. How could a girl not fiend for that tool between her legs? After all, isn't that what Ivy is sniffing around for? His cock is such an addiction and his skills are the drug. I think I've figured it out. I giggle out loud.

"What's so funny, *princess*?" he challenges.

"Nothing. Nothing at all." No way am I telling him about my new found addiction. Or is it an old addiction that I just relapsed with? I double over in laughter when I see his curious stare.

"That's it," he warns. He rushes me and throws me over his shoulder. My jeans dangle from my ankles. He smacks my ass a few times before he slides a couple fingers beneath the fabric of my panties. When he finds my entrance, he thrusts his fingers in me a few times until he has successfully turned me on. The minute I begin to grind against him, the fucker removes them. "Laugh at that, sweetheart."

I love our easy banter. I refuse to let him see just how worked up he has me, though. He lets me down and I continue to get dressed. My giggles are definitely gone though. Score point goes to Diesel.

"Thank you for sending for Brooke. That was so sweet of you," I mention. "I'm sorry I'm just getting around to thanking you. We've been a little preoccupied."

"I try, but you're welcome. I knew you had to be missing her. Besides I would say you thanked the hell out of me, a couple times" he admits. I want to thank him again with my vagina, but I'm afraid that may just increase my raging vagina inferno. My insatiableness knows no bounds right now. I blow him a kiss instead, and head back to the room to be with Brooke. She is laying across the bed with Lily when I enter the room.

"How was it?" Lily asks before I can get a single word out. That damn Brooke. Now these biotches are going too gang up on me.

"Look at that blush," Brooke instigates.

"You two are the nosiest biotches ever," I say, flopping on the bed next to them. "He gave me his cock, I came, the end." I leave out the part about how he managed to make me horny again before sending me on my way.

"Yeah, and you're no fun," Lily rebukes. "You're leaving out all the juicy details. I would tell you all about my nasty sex with Xander, but I'm sure you don't want to hear that."

"Ewww. No way. TMI, Lily. I don't need that mental image in my head."

"See? Just because I can't share doesn't mean you can't. That man is sex on a stick. Just curious if it's all just looks or if he can walk the walk too."

"I already know the answer to that question," Brooke teases. Lily pinches her. "What? I've known her way longer. That was one of the first questions I asked when she started tapping that."

"Hush, Brooke. You are such a dude sometimes. Women don't tap anything. We don't have dicks," Lily retorts. She then looks at me, waiting for the deets.

"Okay fine. Yes. He's the total package. He gorgeous, he has a massive, beautiful cock, and he knows how to use it. The man is both talented and blessed," I conclude.

"Jesus woman. I see why you're all over that," Lily jokes.

"*Mhmm*," Brooke agrees. "I'm surprised you came back. I would have ridden the brakes off that. I love you, but he would have had to pry me off."

"Who says he didn't?" I ask Brooke. "He actually encourage me to come spend some girl time with you before you left, even though I had planned to anyway."

"He's definitely growing on me," she admits. Yeah, me too. It's impossible to just walk away and be his friend again after the mind blowing orgasms and all the sweetness from him. I won't chase him, but just maybe I'm open to being caught, if he wants me. I don't want to get ahead of myself.

There's no reason to believe things will progress past the sex this weekend. No expectations equals no disappointments.

We spend the night gossiping about the sorority girls back on campus, my ideas for the book, and about the homework Lily and I are already behind on. Exhaustion finally consumes me and I fall asleep on their asses.

DIESEL

I'm the first one back on the bus this morning so I use this time to write. I have a new song I've been working on this past week and it is already nearly done. It's another personal one so I hope it's well received by the guys. Another hour passes and those lazy fuckers still haven't made it onto the bus. I grab my bag and head for the shower. Maybe then, I'll feel like meal prepping. I need to get back to that.

I let the water get hot before getting in. As the water hits me, my thoughts wander over Lourdes and this past weekend. I close my eyes and let the stream flow over me.

It's not long before I feel arms wrap around me from behind. I don't have to open my eyes to know that it is Lourdes who has decided to join me in the shower.

"What are you doing, Lourdes?" I ask. Her hand reaches around me and grabs my already half-mast cock. She chooses to show instead of tell. My dick hardens in her hand as she begins to stroke. I let her play for a bit before I grab her wrist. I give a slight tug until she is standing in front of me. The showerhead rains down on us both. She licks her lips and I know that we're on the same page. I take myself into my own hands and watch through hooded lids as she drops to her knees. I rub my dick against her soft, pink lips and she immediately takes me to the back of her throat.

"*Hmmm*," she moans around my cock. I love when she does that. The sensation is incredible. She alternates between teasing the head and playing with my balls. Her tongue darts out to tease that vein on the underside of my dick she likes so much, and I have to brace myself against the shower wall. I grab her head and begin to fuck her face with wild abandon. My control has snapped and she takes every inch of my dick without gagging. My legs stiffen and my hips piston toward my release. She palms my ass and takes me deeper until I cum down her throat. She takes every last drop and then licks her lips again.

"God damn it," I say in total fucking awe. She simply stands up and begins to soap herself down, like she didn't just suck the soul out of my dick.

Seeing her soapy tits, and soap suds running down her hairless pussy, has my shit right back ready to go. One turn deserves another. I push her forward slightly until her hands brace on the travertine in front of her. Her intake of breath spurs me on. I spread her legs and enter her tight pussy from behind.

"My turn, baby," I warn. I slide my dick in and out, taunting her so slowly that her hips begin to buck. I know how she likes it. She wants me to take her hard, deep, and fast. I need her to say it. "Tell me what you want."

"Pleeeeaaaasee, Diesel," she begs.

"As good as it sounds to hear you beg for my dick, I'm going to need the words, baby. Tell me how you want it."

"I need to you dee...deeper," she stutters. I deepen my strokes. "Faster...harder, please, Diesel."

And there it is. I slam into her over and over again. Her pussy clenches around my dick to milk every thrust. I'm so close again and I need her to get there. She's on the brink. I can feel it. I reach around her and rub her clit while my dick goes deeper still. I then pull the triumph card that shatters the rest of her control.

"Feel me deep in your pussy baby. Feel how hard you make me. I'm getting ready to come in this pussy that belongs to me, so let go. Come on your dick, baby. It's yours." My filthy mouth. It gets her every time. She fucking squirts all over my dick like a waterfall. I let my own release go and cum with her. We ride the wave together. That may be our hardest orgasm together yet. "Shit" is all I can say. We hear talking outside the bus and reality comes crashing down around us. The guys are getting ready to load the bus. I grab the soap to reluctantly wash her off of my dick as quickly as I can. I leave her in the shower so I can get the hell out of this bathroom before we're caught. I dry off in record time and throw on a pair basketball shorts before they even board the bus. Thank God Reckless Ambition held them up. I don't even know what they were discussing and I don't care. That was close. I'm going to have to be more careful than that.

CHAPTER
Eighteen

DIESEL

WE'RE BACK ON THE ROAD AND HEADING TOWARD Texas. We've kind of settled back into status quo with everyone off in a little space they've claimed for themselves, but all I can think about is Lourdes. When did I let her back in? I can't even blame it on our earth shattering sex because I suspect that she never left my heart.

I sit here at our dinner slash card table wishing I could go to her. I don't want to put a title on it because that just screws everything up, but I can't deny it anymore, I need her in my life. We have a record deal, we're already beginning to climb the charts, and it seems like the world is our oyster right now. Yet I can't help but feel like she is the one piece that is missing. And since I can't offer her a relationship, I can't even approach Xander about us. The whole thing is so complicated. I watch her lying across her bunk, biting her lip like she does when she's deep in thought. I see the Algebra book she has open and suddenly I have my excuse to go to her.

I plop on the small bunk next to her. She looks up at me in surprise before looking around nervously to see where Xander is.

"Relax, princess. You look like you could use some help over here," I say, pointing to her math book. She turns over on her back and grins up at me. Those fucking beautiful grays of hers send a punch to my gut.

"That obvious, huh?" She makes room on the bunk for me. "They just want our money. I don't even need this class for my career path, yet they make everybody take these core classes."

"Well, good thing I just happen to be good at math," I say, smirking. "I can be your private tutor." I draw tiny circles on her wrist with my finger. The look that passes between us is electric.

"I'm just a little ole' poor college student," she drawls out, eager to play along.

"Oh, I bet I could think of some ways for you to pay off your debt." I wink. She tries to hold it in at first, but fails. She laughs so loud, it gets the attention of our guys. I don't miss the curious stare from Xander in particular.

I don't even care. I fucking love that sound coming from her, especially since I was the one to break her before. Her laugh is the most amazing sound to my ears. I ignore the attention on us and begin to tickle her. She laughs even harder until her cute little ass wiggles right out of the bed and onto the floor.

I don't want Xander to blow a coronary so I get up to go join the guys, but I help her up first. "We'll talk about the terms of my tutoring later, princess," I whisper before I go. She is all smiles as she climbs back into her bunk to try and resume her studying *Good luck with that*. I can't help my own smile that forms knowing she's thinking about me now, too, if she wasn't already.

"What was that all about?" Xander asks when I sit down on the sofa next to him and Lily. Lily hides her own smile behind her shirt sleeve and I know instantly she knows. Lourdes has been talking it seems. Hmmm, good things I hope. The blush trailing up Lily's neck is an indication that it was.

"Oh, just teasing your sis for sucking at math. I happen to be a math genius you know?" I wink at Lily because I know she sees through my bullshit. If Lourdes trusted her enough to tell her anything about us then I know that I can too.

"Well, that definitely explains the laughter," Xander chuckles. "Damn self-proclaimed genius," he adds. If only he knew. The guys may think that music was the only gift I was given, and I'm fine with letting them believe exactly that.

"Hey, I have an idea for another cover song for our next concert if you guys can learn if before we get to Texas," I mention to change the subject. Honestly the song is an old favorite, but the fact that it popped into my head when I was tickling Lourdes makes me want to perform it.

The mention of a new song has his attention. He calls for Keyser and Gable to come hear about it.

"This new song…is it something we can rock out to or a

ballad?" Gable asks. The guys know I like to keep us diverse. We can rock with any song, but sometimes we like to slow things down and give the audience some our tenderness to keep them guessing.

"A ballad, but one that is open for interpretation. It can be about love, a personal struggle, redemption, or whatever the listener identifies it to be," I explain.

"Sounds deep, man. What is it?" Keyser joins in on the conversation.

"*The Unknown* by Dirty South featuring Fmlybnd," I tell them, but I see the confused expressions on their faces. "You guys need to broaden the genres you listen to. Xander, grab me your guitar and a mic." He shoots me the finger but then gets up to get what I asked for. I see Lourdes close her laptop. She joins us in the living area to hear me play. She's the inspiration for wanting to do this cover so I want her to hear me.

"Here you go, since you asked so kindly," Xander says handing the mic and guitar to me.

Since I can't play and hold the mic at the same time I pass it to Lourdes.

"Lourdes do you mind holding the mic so I don't have to find a stand for this thing?" She takes the mic from me and nods nervously. It's cute. Wait until she hears the lyrics. I'm going to sing to her in front of the entire bus and enjoy her reaction when she realizes why I picked this song.

"*Head shaking, heart racing, thick fear is all around. A wall of darkness in front of me,*" I sing, looking into Lourdes's eyes. Recognition of the lyrics is apparent. Her eyes begin to water before I even make it to the chorus. Thankfully, Lily is tearing up too. It keeps the guys from figuring out the significance. "*Dive deep to the unknown*," I repeat over and over. I close my own eyes as the chorus resonates so deeply with what I'm feeling right now. I don't have all the answers— whether I should stay away from the one woman who has the power to destroy me or embrace the fall of the unknown. This song coming to me when it did tells me I should just dive deep into the unknown.

"I freaking love it," Xander says after I sing the last lyric. "It's definitely a song that will move the crowd. I can't wait to bring in all the instrumentals. It even has the girls crying."

"Yeah, man. What made you think of it?" Gable presses. His piercing stare is telling. He's trying to figure out if I really just laid my feeling out about Lourdes for everyone to see. The answer to that was received by its intended recipient, so he can just keep wondering. I love my guys like they are my brothers, but somethings I can't share.

"I don't know, Gable. I guess having my brother visit just kicked up a lot of past history and unresolved shit simmering at the surface. Like I said, this song is about individual inter- pretation." He and Keyser nod their understanding so I guess my explanation is satisfactory.

Thing is, everything I said is true. My past is the reason for my mistrust. I've experienced firsthand how fickle love is. All the shit that I try to suppress is never far from the sur- face—there threatening to be seen...to be exposed.

"I have one more song about redemption," I tell the guys. "I wrote this one and have laid the tracks to it, but we can tweak it later." If they thought the first song was something, this one is even more revealing. So much so, I hesitated if I should share it or not. Throwing caution to the wind, I begin.

I told myself that I'd never look back
I was the reason for all your pain and I never wanted
*   to hurt you again*
I never wanted to be the reason for your tears so it
*   was best that I moved on*

But then you forgave me for all my past sins
You refused to give my heart back and it was then
*   that the road to my redemption began*

Here is my creed of Redemption
I promise to be a better man this time around
My heart was never mine from the minute you came
*   around*

Here is my creed of redemption
I will give you my all
You've seen me at my worst
You see me like nobody else can
You have my heart and I will forever be your man

Redemption
Redemption
You're my redemption

The guys applaud and tell me how badass they think the song is, but I can only focus on Lourdes. What is she thinking? She will always have my heart and I know this now. My thoughts are interrupted by Lourdes handing me back the mic. She wipes away her tears with the back of her hands.

"That was beautiful, Diesel," she says as she looks away. I don't want her to look away. I want to see the feelings that she's hiding. I want to kiss her tears away and dive deep within her. Instead I have to watch her walk away. She climbs back into her bunk, but she doesn't open her laptop this time. She moves the book out of her way. She turns so that her back is facing us and I fucking hate that I can't go to her.

I get up to get myself a glass of water. The guys are still discussing the songs and their take on it. Lily comes up to me and puts a hand on my shoulder. I jump from the shock of her touch. I wasn't expecting it.

"I got it, Diesel, and so did Lourdes. That was fucking beautiful. Ballsy, but beautiful," she says. "I'll go and talk to her. I think I know what she may be feeling right now." I knew Lourdes had told her about us and now she just confirmed it. I don't know how much she knows, but I'm glad Lourdes has someone to confide in.

"What is that, Lily? What is it that you think she's feeling?" I look to make sure the guys are not listening to us, but they're not.

"Well, if I just had the man that I have feelings for sing a song like that to me in front of everyone and I couldn't react, I'd be pretty bummed about it. I'm not inside her head Diesel, but if I had to guess, I'd say she's sad that she can't just be with you." I never thought about that. Lily is nearly out of the kitchen before I answer her.

"Same." I shake my head. "Fucking same."

Lourdes

"Hey," I hear Lily whisper behind me. She climbs onto my bunk with me and I look up at her through teary eyes. "Aww, Lourdes. Come on. Let's go talk." I don't want to get up, but she's not having it. I don't want to cause a scene so I follow her. She throws her head back in laughter like I've just said the funniest thing ever. I'm guessing we're being watched. Once we're behind closed doors, she pulls me into hug. I let the sobs wrack my body.

"It's not fair, Lily. Happiness has always been just out of reach for me. Sometimes I don't even feel like I'm alive—like I'm just existing, you know?" She hugs me tighter and I let it all go. "I watch everyone else in their own happiness, but I can't seem to have any for myself. Something always happens, and now this. Diesel practically admitted that he still has feelings for me with that song. He doesn't let people in, Lily. Neither of us can do jack shit about it without the risk of unraveling everything the band has worked so hard to build."

"I'm so sorry. Maybe I could talk to Xander. He's the key to this shit storm, right? If he was on board with you two being together then Keyser and Gable would have no reason to care." I can see the concern etched in her face.

"It would never work, and I couldn't gamble the band's future on him understanding. Too much has happened. He witnessed me going from his princess to what he called Goth Barbie. I transformed into an introvert who was only a shell of the girl he once knew. He had always been over protective of me, but even more so when he saw the change. He even speculated that some douche had broken my heart. You saw how Diesel was at the beginning of this tour with Ivy and then Melissa. You think my brother would willingly give him the green light to be with me? Not to mention the shit he probably has inside knowledge of that I have no idea about."

Lily takes a seat on the bed and pats a spot next to her. "I know you're right. I just wish there was a way," she agrees sadly.

"Me too. I didn't come here for Diesel. I really didn't. We're like magnets. When we're in the vicinity of each other, we can't resist the pull." My tears fall harder. "Maybe I should just leave. We're both stronger apart."

"No way. You're not leaving. I'll do what I can to cover for you guys," Lily pleads. I guess I said that out loud. "Look we will think of something to get you two some alone time until you can figure out a better plan."

"I can't ask you to do that Lily. If this all comes out, and Xander finds out that you not only knew, but had hand in us being together, he will feel betrayed. He may not forgive you."

"I get that and it's not a betrayal. I love you both. You're his sister and you need me too, Lourdes. We all need to feel like we have somebody. I know you have Brooke, but guess what? You have me too, and I say just existing is not a way for anyone to live. If Diesel is the man that makes you feel alive, then it is not up to anyone else to dispute that. If Xander ever finds out, I'll just have to make him see that I did this out of my love for you He loves you, Lourdes. I talked to him briefly before I came to you. He's sad too. You two need each other and I plan to do everything in my power to make sure the two of you have a chance."

Lily has said a mouth full. I know I should insist again that she stay out of this, but she is just as intense as Brooke. Her intentions are pure and sweet and frankly we could use her help. She's right. Diesel is the only man that makes me feel alive—my skeletons don't seem so suffocating when everything is right between us. I need him.

"Okay," I whisper.

"Okay," she agrees. She scoots further up the bed and folds down the covers for me. "Everything is going to be all right. I'm here, Lourdes." That's all she needs to say. There is no way I can go back out there without drawing suspicion and there is no way Diesel can come in here to comfort me for the exact same reason. Lily turns out the lights and I know that she's not going to leave me. For the first time since this tour began, I'm hopeful. I may not be able to have the relationship that I want with Diesel, but with Lily's help it will be more than nothing. That's a start. I'll take something over nothing.

CHAPTER
Nineteen

Lourdes

THE LAST FEW DAYS WITH DIESEL HAVE BEEN AMAZING. We sneak little kisses in when nobody is watching or early morning touching before everyone else gets up. Our constant flirting is giving me a blue vagina though. Still, I appreciate the time we get. This is the Diesel that I fell for—the tender moments that eradicate witnessing him being a manwhore. Although, we haven't put a label on what we're doing, it feels like old times. We're teetering on dangerous ground, but I have never felt more alive. I'm addicted to this feeling—this high. I'm addicted to him and I can finally admit that to myself.

He is in his bunk above mine now, but since Xander is in

his with Lily right across from us, I don't make any attempts to mess with him. His phone rings and I hear him answer.

"Yeah, Sevyn. What's up, man?" Diesel lowers his voice, but I can still hear him. "What? I wonder how in the hell they found out? This is good, though, right?" He pauses and I wish I could hear what is being said. I know I shouldn't be eavesdropping, but something is up. "Okay. Look into it and let me know when you have something," he finishes before ending the call.

"Everything all right?" Xander questions from across the way.

"Just peachy," Diesel remarks. He hops from his bunk when the bus begins to come to a stop and I see that he is shirtless. I watch his muscles flex as he pulls a t-shirt from the place he was just lying and slips it over his head. I want to sneak in a touch so bad. I need to tide over this hunger for him. He looks down at me and smirks. *Handsome Fucker.* I stick my tongue out at him.

"Give your girl a breather and come rehearse slacker," he tells Xander. He walls off, but not before winking at me. I swear it's one of his hottest Dieselisms. That and his signature smirk. Xander kisses Lily before he gets up to follow Diesel and a pang of jealousy hits me. I wish we could be just as open. I'd be lying if I said I wasn't envious of his relationship with Lily. Those two are so perfect for one another. As soon as he is out of sight, she comes over to my bunk.

"Want to watch some reality TV and make fun of the stupid crap they do?" I'm caught up on homework and I've already written some for the book. I don't watch television that often, but a distraction is in order.

"Sure. I need your help with this grocery list first if you don't mind. Xander asked if we could get the stuff on the list they made while they rehearse," Lily mentions. "The list is not too bad."

"You know I don't mind. It'll help cut the time in half if we split the list." I'm already out of my bunk. "So they're not getting off the bus at all?" We've haven't reached our next scheduled stop, but sometimes Gus and Stewart will stop to take a break from driving and to allow us to get things we need.

"Yeah. They're getting off to rehearse on Reckless Ambition's bus," Lily says. She's looking through the refrigerator to see if the guys forgot to put anything on the list. She writes some things on the paper she has in her hand while I peek out of the window. The guys are already gone.

I see the sleek black bus parallel to ours. Both buses purposefully leave off any identifying signage revealing who's inside. The other bus is always either in front or behind us, but Reckless Ambition is rarely on it. They travel by flight and stay in hotels mostly. Their bus just carries their equipment to each tour stop.

"I bet the interior of their bus is even nicer than this one," I say, still staring out the window.

"I'm sure it is. It's the *party bus*." Lily pauses and tries to change the subject. "Are you ready to go?"

"What do you mean by party bus?" I'm not letting her off the hook. Apparently Xander shares with her way more than he does with me. She looks at me hesitantly. "Spill it, Lily."

"Sometimes the guys get off the bus, Lourdes. We stop

long enough for them to get on the other bus before we start moving again. That's where all the groupie shit happens. Since the other band is rarely on there, it's a place for them to be wild without subjecting us to their sexual conduct."

My jaw drops in shock. I think back to all the times the bus seemed empty, but I just naively assumed that they were up front or in their bunks. "Xander told you all of this?" I question.

"Yeah. I only know because I woke up in the middle of the night and he was nowhere to be found. I didn't understand since we were still moving. When I messaged him he told me he was on the other bus. I made him come clean about what was going on. He promised me that he didn't do anything. He was just hanging with the guys. He even said he wouldn't go back on there if I didn't want him too."

"Why would you keep this from me?" Our guys have been creeping out at night for some extracurricular activity and I didn't even know about it. We've been on the road for a few weeks now and I didn't think the guys were living out the full experience. I thought they were keeping things tame for our sake, and they were. They just moved shit to another bus. Well played Xander. I know he's behind this. "Lily?"

"I'm sorry, Lourdes. It really has been a while since the guys visited the other bus. Last night was the first time since before our conversation." Then it hits me. What's she's not saying.

"Diesel went on the other bus last night? After I was asleep?" The conversation she is referring to is when she said she would cover for Diesel and me if needed. The fact that she didn't say anything means she thinks he was screwing someone else on that bus.

"I'm sure it was nothing," she explains. "It's just their time away from the estrogen on this bus."

"Really? Did Xander go too?" She shakes her head no, and I can feel my face getting hot. Diesel has been flirting with me like crazy. The sexual tension between us has been off the charts, only he's had a way to release his. Why wouldn't he fuck someone else? I want to storm that other bus and demand he tell me what game he's playing. He sang that fucking song for me and gets me all emotionally invested again only to go do God knows what on the fucking groupie bus. Tears stream down my face and I don't bother wiping them away. "You should have told me Lily. I thought you said that I had you. I thought you said you were my friend."

"That's not fair. I'm your friend." She tries to reach for me, but I step back. "You don't know if anything happened. Reckless Ambition is on the bus so maybe they just hung out last night"

"So why didn't Xander go? Answer that. He didn't want to piss you off because I'm sure he knew exactly what was going down on the other bus. My God. Fucking Ivy is over there. The one person who has made it known that she fucked Diesel." My tears fall harder at the cracking of my voice. I feel so stupid right now.

"Please Lourdes—" Lily tries, but I flip her off. A real friend wouldn't let me look stupid.

"Go to the store by yourself. Ask Gus or Stewart to help you. I'm done."

I don't stick around for her response. I leave her standing there. I retreat to the bedroom and slam the door. Once

I'm behind closed doors, I allow myself to fall apart. It's true what they say about highs. What goes up, eventually comes down—except I've fucking come crashing down. Now I've trapped myself in the very room with all of our damn memories. I take a seat on the floor on the other side of the bed and bring my knees to my chest. Sobs wrack my body from the unfairness of it all. I know I can't expect him to wait around for me when there is an invitation to pussy right on the next bus.

I don't know how long I'm on the floor balling my eyes out before there is a bang on the door. "Lourdes, open this damn door." It's Diesel. So now Lily decides to have a big mouth. I don't move from my spot here on the floor, nor do I answer him. "I swear I will break this fucking door down. Either open it now or we'll both have some explaining to do—your choice."

I don't know what all Lily told him, but he has some nerve. Fuck him. He wants in here so bad, then so be it. I'll leave. I pull myself off the floor and open the door. I try to storm past him, but he pushes his way in and slams the door behind him.

"What the fuck? You got something you want to ask me?" he huffs. He's pissed, but so am I.

"I don't have shit to ask you," I retort. I try again to move past him, but he grabs me by the wrists.

"I'm not going to let you fucking do this. Not this time." His eyes pin me to the spot.

"Not going to let me do what, Diesel?" Fresh tears trail down the path of the dried ones. I see his eyes soften, but I don't want his pity.

"Run. I'm not going to let you run from me again. Since you won't ask, then I'll tell you. Yes. I joined the guys on the other bus last night. We just talked shit and hung out. Yes, there was groupie pussy in the mix, but I didn't partake. Ivy didn't join the guys until this morning, but even if she had been on the bus, I wouldn't have fucked her either. Don't you get it yet?" He wipes my tears and kisses me softly on the lips. I want to hold on to the anger. Deep down, I feel like he's telling me the truth, so why is it so hard to let it go? "I know what you need," he whispers.

He tries to deepen the kiss, but I don't let him in. He steps back and pulls his shirt off over his head. My traitorous eyes peruse his body. He takes my hands and puts them on the button of his jeans after he locks the door.

"Take what's yours, Lourdes. Free your cock, baby. It's been waiting for you and only you." His words shatter my resolve. My nimble fingers undo the button. I don't even ask about the guys. I don't care if we get caught. I need this hurt to go away. I unzip him and free his already hard cock from confinement. As usual, he's commando. The urge to take him into my mouth is the same every time I get a look at how beautiful it is. I drop to my knees, but he pulls me back up. "I said I know what you need. Let me show you."

When I don't move he begins to undress me slowly. It doesn't take him long to rid me of my ratty t-shirt and leggings. I try to help him by removing my panties and bra, but he stills my hands. "What—" I begin, and he silences me with a single finger to my lips.

"Leave them. I like the white lace. So innocent looking, but what I want to do to you is anything but." He smirks wickedly. "Get on the bed. I'm going to fuck any doubt you may have right out of your mind." He's standing there with his jeans open and his hand around his cock. He strokes himself, and I'm hypnotized by the act. It's so fucking hot. I get on the bed, getting wetter by the minute watching him. "Now lie back and massage your clit. I want to see you play."

I don't know if I can do this. He wants to watch me masturbate? "Come on, baby," I hear him say. His voice encourages me to let go so I lay back and close my eyes. "That's it." His lust spurs me on. My hands inch toward the spot where he wants them. I've never had an audience so I'm a little nervous. I rub my clit slowly, trying to think about Diesel's eyes on me. With my own eyes closed, I try to imagine that I'm alone in this room.

"*Mmmm*," I moan. With each pass of my finger, it becomes slicker.

"Holy fuck, baby," Diesel growls. "I thought I could just watch for a bit but, fuck, I can't." He peels off his jeans and in an instant my legs surround his waist. He slams into me and there is no build up. He fucks me savagely, driving deeper with each stroke. He leans down and take my mouth in a punishing kiss as we both race toward our orgasms. I palm his ass to make him go even deeper.

"Dieseeeel…" I come so hard around his cock that I milk his release from him too. I can feel him throbbing inside me. My legs begin to tremble and it's as if my orgasm rolls on and on. We lay there motionless for several minutes with him still inside. When he finally pulls out, I feel bereft. I want to hold on to this moment. I don't want to go back to pretending for the guys. I grab his arm and I know he feels it too.

"I have to go, baby. Lily convinced the guys that they had too much shit on their list for her to get, after she texted me and told me that you were upset. I knew she was creating a window for us to talk," Diesel shares.

"Except we haven't gotten much talking done," I point out. I may have been a little hard on Lily. It's like I'm just waiting for the other shoe to drop—waiting for Diesel to grow bored with the secrecy and move on. I took that out on her because I couldn't address the real issue.

"Didn't need much talking. All you need to know is that you don't have anything to worry about. I'm not labeling anything, but I only want you. My dick wants you, too, so I'll just let him do the talking for now," he jokes. "But seriously, I need to get back to the store before they start checking out. Can I get you anything?"

"Nope. I'm good. I just got what I wanted," I assure him. This is what I needed. I needed his reassurance. We don't have to put a title on it. Knowing that he wants me is enough. I'm okay with taking things slow. Our past makes it hard to trust, but if we're meant to be together it will happen. For now, I just want this with him. Whatever *"this"* is.

"Good. No doubts, okay? If anything ever changes, I'll let you know. What I want is on this bus not the other way around," he assures. He kisses me on the forehead before cleaning himself up in the bathroom. When he leaves, I go and draw myself a bath. I'm not ready to leave our bubble.

CHAPTER
Twenty

DIESEL

'M HELPING THE GUYS PUT THE GROCERIES AWAY WHEN I look over at the television and see my face on it. Not only mine, but Sevyn is right next to me on the screen. *What the fuck?*

"Hey, turn that up," Xander tells Lourdes, who is closest to the television. I can't find my fucking phone fast enough to call Sevyn. It rings in my hand as I pull it out of my pocket. I see that he is calling me.

"Are you watching the news?" I ask before he can get any words out.

"Yeah. I don't know what to do. It's all out, man. The whole fucking plan," he swears.

"Where are you now?" I have to think of something quick. I'm only catching the end of the news, but I know it's bad. The fucking headlines read Twins plotting to takeover Beck Investments. How in the hell did this get out?

"I had just left the office. I can't go back now. Our father is due back tomorrow and I pretty sure he has already gotten the call," Sevyn says. "What the hell are we going to do?"

"Right now we need to just get you here. Don't go back to the office and don't say shit to anyone. Stay away from the reporters." We decide that he is going to meet us in Houston since we're almost there. We're supposed to have a show there tomorrow night.

"What the hell is going on?" Gable asks once I end the call with my brother.

I have no choice but to try to fix this. I have to come clean because now my face is all over the media. I don't know how much of our plan is blown, but I have to get in front of this.

"Sevyn and I had a plan to take over our father's company," I begin and the room goes quiet. Keyser turns off the TV.

"Tell us everything, man," he encourages. I don't want to keep telling my fucked-up story, but they're involved now. I've brought the band into this mess. I sit down on the sofa and they take seats around me. I know I need to come clean now, but I hate reliving this shit. I hate having to tell them I'm the fucking son that Claude didn't want—the fuck up that couldn't do anything right. I don't want to admit I got thrown out on my ass at the age of seventeen. It fucking destroyed me. The D/s shit that Melissa introduced me to saved my life. I was able to take control over my life back. It kept me from acting out, getting into drugs or gangs. I had another outlet. They don't need to know all of that, but this whole fucking story takes me back to a place I don't want to visit.

I sit here with my head in my hands. Just thinking about this shit being exposed for the world to see has me seeing red. I don't need people's fucking judgments or pity. My eyes are closed, but I can feel them waiting for me to tell them what's going on.

Then I feel her hands on my back. The gesture is simple yet comforting. "Let's give him some time, guys. He'll tell us when he's ready," I hear Lourdes say. "Diesel, you don't have to do this now. We can wait." She knows some of the story but not all of it. I didn't tell her about Melissa or the plan I had in place with my brother. All she knows about is the abandonment part. I don't say shit. I just sit here unable to move. The weight of my reality sits heavy on my shoulders.

"I agree," Lily seconds.

"We'll be back. Come on Diesel," she says pulling me up. I let her, but then I try to let go of her hand. I don't think she realizes how this looks.

"It's okay, Lourdes. I just need a minute." I try again to remove my hand from hers but she clenches tighter.

"Nonsense—" she insists, but Xander cuts her off.

"Lourdes, what are you doing? He's telling you nicely that he needs a minute. Let him go." She drops my hand and her gaze falls to the floor.

"Sorry," she says softly. "I was just trying to be a friend."

"You're fine. Thank you, but I just need a breather. That's all. Fuck it though." I need to get the attention off of Lourdes and myself. Her open concern for me just cast suspicion overs us. I see it in Xander's questioning stare. If I leave this room and she follows me, we're busted.

I divulge my freaking teen years that helped to form my demons. I tell them about Claude giving Sevyn controlling shares of the company and our plan to share ownership. I wasn't going to leave the band. We just wanted to own the company equally. I tell them everything with the exception of Melissa and the role she plays in all of this.

"I don't understand," Xander speaks up. At least his mind seems to be off of us. "Wouldn't our fame mess up that plan?"

"No. First of all. We're not famous yet so Sevyn and I could still fly under the radar. We were planning to execute our plan before our father came home—long before the band reached stardom. Someone had already leaked that Claude was sick a couple days ago and that was great. It meant that we didn't have to do it. The focus was supposed to be on the fact that he was sick and was trying to bring someone else into the company."

"I agree. It's all so confusing," Keyser says.

"It's public knowledge that Claude has two sons—twin sons. He couldn't hide that even if he wanted to. The upset to the plan is that nobody knew, not even him, the extent to which we merged our identities. What started off as a ploy to get me unquestioned access to our home to visit with my mother, transformed into a plan to have me take my rightful seat next to my brother on the throne, if you will. I never cared for the company like Sevyn. It was never my dream, but it is his. He would have forfeited his inheritance of the company out of guilt if I refused to own it with him." I sit back down on the sofa.

"So, I said yes," I admit. "Partly out of the love for my brother and partly as revenge on Claude. I wanted to see his face when he realized the son he didn't want owned part of the company he willingly gave to the other son. Don't you get it? This hurts my brother more than me. I just don't want the media digging up past shit. Sevyn on the other hand, cares. He didn't want the betrayal to come from him, once he found out that Claude was dying. It was never supposed to come out this way. It was one thing for him to announce me as the other owner, but for the world to know the deceit and scheming that took place behind the scenes to get me there, is another. It will crush our father, and Sevyn, in the process."

"Damn," Gable sighs. "That is cold blooded. Not that your father didn't deserve this, but I can see Sevyn's side of it. Here's a man at death's door who gives all of his controlling shares in his company to who he thinks is the good son, and then learns that the good son has been plotting with the other son to unravel his plan for him to be the sole owner. This is some TV type shit for real."

"Gable!" They all yell at him.

"What?" He shakes his head. "I'm just saying I understand now. No shade. I'm here for you man. I do get your side too. You were robbed of part of your childhood with him. Your brother felt that honor should not have been placed upon him without you. You both are the victims here. Not your dad. This should have never come to pass." He surprises me by patting me on the back.

"Enough of that. I don't want to keep thinking about it right now. Sevyn is flying in tonight and we'll figure out a way to spin this. I just didn't want you guys to be blindsided by our personal crap. Claude is not the most well liked. Some of his hostile takeovers have earned him quite a few enemies. The press is going to have a field day with this one. I'll need to warn Desiree, too."

"Yeah. Surprised we haven't heard from her yet," Keyser agrees. "Whatever. We're going to rock Houston tomorrow night like none of this shit matters."

"Fuck, yes. That's what I'm saying," Gable echoes. The girls have been pretty quiet, but Lourdes's expression is telling. She's worried about me. I give her a small wink when the others are not looking. She smiles and it's what I need in this chaos. Everything is going to be okay.

Sevyn walks through the door after what seems like a freaking eternity. Gus left to pick him up from the airport ages ago. There is no smile greeting me this time. His solemn affect is ominous. Xander must see it too.

"Why don't you two talk in the bedroom?" he suggests. "Decide how you're going to handle this and then let us know what we can do to help."

"Thanks, man," I acknowledge and I'm already heading toward the room.

"Of course," he says behind me.

I close the door behind Sevyn and motion for him to take a seat. "Why the face man. What is it?"

"Diesel. I'm so sorry." Something is wrong. More than what just happened on the news.

"What the hell is it? Just tell me."

"It was Melissa," he rushes out.

"What about her?" He isn't making any sense.

"She's behind the leak. She was in the bathroom when we talked, remember?" His eyes cast downward in remorse.

I see red at his accusation. "You're wrong. I know it all seems coincidental, but she would never do that. You don't know her like I do or the things she's helped me through. She would never betray me like that." He shakes his head like he is trying to clear it.

"No, you're wrong brother. I do know her like you do. *Exactly* like you do," he emphasizes. What the hell is he saying? My heart quickens because I hope he's not saying what I think he is. "She confessed to me that she did it. First she leaked that our father was sick. Next she leaked that his twin sons were plotting to pull his business right from under him. Her last card is her ace. One, neither one of us wants her to play." My worst fear is being realized. I know what he is going to tell me. My fucking demons already have one foot out the door, tap dancing in the light.

"Her ace? What is it Sevyn?"

"She was my submissive, brother. Same as she was yours. We're being blackmailed." And there it is. Our truths. Identical right down to our demons.

We are the pawns in our own game. The air I breathe is suffocating. The very relationship that gave me strength at a time when I needed it the most, was a lie. Melissa betrayed me. Which of us was first? What was the angle? Then another reality comes crashing down on me. Sevyn knew. When he was here a couple weeks ago and Melissa was here with me, he knew then, if not before.

"You knew. God damn it. Before she leaked any of this, you knew that we were messing with the same woman when you saw her on this bus and you were willing to let her betray me even further."

"Diesel, I—" I cut him off. If he says another word, I will not be responsible for my actions. How can I fucking trust people when everyone who I ever loved or let close to me fucked me over? My father. Women. And now my own twin brother. I punch the fucking wall to keep from crushing his face. The frame caves and blood drips down my knuckles.

The guys try to ask me what is wrong when they see me come out, but Xander motions for them to get the hell out my way. I go up to the front of the bus and tell Stewart to stop this fucking bus. I need off and now! I'm guessing Stewart feels the shit storm I have brewing so he doesn't question my request. He assures me that he'll take the next exit and find somewhere to stop.

I return to the living area to throw on some shoes. Nobody dares to try to talk with me, except Lourdes that is.

"Is everything okay?"

What kind of fucked-up question is that? Do I look okay to her? "Since you missed the context clues of me being pissed, *princess*, no. I'm not fucking okay!" Xander is on my ass in a heartbeat.

"I don't give a shit what's going on in your life. You will not take that shit out on my sister." We are nose to nose.

"Xander, it's okay. We're here for you, Diesel," she says grabbing the hand that is bloody. I pull it away from her.

"It's not okay because I just found out that I can't trust a Single. Fucking. Person." I yell.

"You can trust me," she says softly not realizing she just said "me" instead of "us."

The bus comes to a rolling stop. I look around the bus at all of the stares. Then I look at Lourdes and the tears that threaten to fall from her eyes send me over the edge. She left me once too. She has played a part in hurting me.

"Really? I can trust you, Lourdes?" She nods. "How can I trust you when you can't even tell your stepbrother that you're fucking me!" I don't even see Xander's fist coming. He gets one jab into my mouth before the guys pull him off me. I wipe the blood away and look over at Lourdes. She is full on crying now and Xander is fighting to get free.

And that, ladies and gentleman, is how you make a fucking exit. *Fuck this!*

Sneak Peek of *Unforbidden*
(Forbidden Trilogy) ~ Book # 3
By: S.R. Watson

Chapter 1

Footsteps sound above me, but that is all I can decipher. My eyes strain to take in my surroundings, but I'm in pitch blackness. The smell of urine is so prevalent, I struggle to keep down the bile that is threatening to come up. I feel around the springy fabric I'm lying on, that I'm guessing is a mattress. I get up on all fours and crawl slowly until I'm completely off the pungent smelling thing. I come in contact with cold concrete. Where the hell am I? A sliver of panic crosses me as I come to the realization that I have to be in a basement of some sort. There are no basements in California. Oh God, how will anyone ever find me? I let my guard down and my stalker got to me. How many days have passed? I'm scared and pissed off at the same time. What is this sick fuck going to do with me? So many questions are going through my mind at warp speed. Surely Grayson has realized I'm missing by now, and I'm sure Jordan will tell him and my mom everything.

The footsteps grow louder. Someone is coming. I swallow the lump in my throat as I work to gather my courage. Maybe I can run once he opens the door, only I don't know which way the door is yet so I'll have to be quick. He won't be expecting me to be awake or me running. The door creaks open and I get ready to make my escape.

Holy crap! There are two of them. My moment of hesitation relinquishes my perceived advantage. I attempt to sprint past them anyway, but I'm easily caught. The door ahead seems miles away.

"Not so fast," the blond man chastises. His grip on my arms tells me he means business. His lip curls as he snarls. "There is nowhere to run to, doll. Even if you manage to escape this house, we're in the middle of nowhere." I pull against him and he belts out a hearty laugh.

"That is enough, Roc," the darker haired man warns. "Let her go. She isn't going anywhere." So the blond's name is Roc—not a real name, I'm sure. Hell, what does it matter? I've seen their faces. What is their plan for me? More importantly, what will they do with me after I'm no longer useful?

"Why am I here?" I manage to speak up.

"You're going to make us a lot of money, sweetness," Roc says as he uses one finger to caress the side of my arm. I shiver at his dirty touch and then I see it. The scorpion tattoo on his hand. It looks familiar to me.

"Cut the shit, Roc. Let's do what we came down here to do." The dark haired guy seems to be more sensible, then again he is part of this kidnapping. I'm guessing I'm being held for ransom. "Put this over your head Siobhan," he says as he hands me some kind of pillowcase.

Dark haired man, who has yet to be identified, knows my name. *What the fuck?* "How do you know my name?" I challenge.

"I know a lot. Now just put the pillow case over your head so we can bring you upstairs," he says.

"Fuck this!" Roc snatches the pillow case from me and

puts it over my head before pulling my arms behind my back. "You're being too nice to this bitch, and she doesn't respect the situation she's in." I pull against him, but his grip tightens.

"You don't have to be a dick, Roc. Let's just take her upstairs."

Dark haired guy is both taller and more muscular than Roc, but it seems as though Roc is the one in charge. Roc nudges me forward as an indication to start walking. I can't see where the hell I'm going, so he is leading me with one hand gripping my arm and the other holding the pillowcase so it doesn't slip off. We go up some stairs to reach floor level of the house and then another couple of flights after we're inside. The fucker purposefully let me bump into a couple of corners and it hurts like a bitch. After a few turns, I'm shoved into a room and the door is slammed shut. I hear a few locks being turned from the other side of the door. I wait a few seconds and take the pillowcase off. There is actually light in here. I look around to assess my surroundings. It's a bedroom, if you can call it that. It has a single twin size bed with sheets, a comforter, and a pillow. The Disney Princesses stares back at me from the pink, girly comforter. How ironic? I damn sure don't feel like a princess right now.

Anything is a step up from that smelly mattress in the basement though. I'm so glad I couldn't see what it looked like in the darkness. Aside from the bed, there's not much else in here. There is a single chair against the wall and the one window is boarded up. What was the point of bringing me up here? I walk over and sit on the edge of the bed, wired with unanswered questions. Time seems to stand still, yet I don't know how many days have passed. My thoughts are interrupted when I hear the door being unlocked. Blondie walks in and pushes the door closed ominously. His sneer is threatening as he motions toward the chair.

"Have a seat over here," he says as he pulls the chair to the center of the room. I stare at him blankly, wondering what the heck he is up to. "Hurry up bitch. I'm not Alex. I will not tolerate disobedience." Ah, dark haired guy finally has a name. This disclosure worries me because I know too much. I watch television. I know how these things end. They're probably going to kill me after they get what they want. I get up and walk slowly to the chair. If they're going to kill me anyway, why make things easier for them. My defiance is met with a body slam into the chair. The chair tips slightly as my weight is thrown against the wooden frame.

"Don't test me!" Roc spits. My arm aches from the blunt force of the chair. I try not to wince and give this fucker the satisfaction.

Roc straddles my thighs and bears his weight on my lap. His hand tangles in my hair as he yanks my head back. His face is mere inches from mine. His breath is suffocating me as I work to control my own respirations. I start to hyperventilate in panic.

"I will fuck you up, doll, or I could just fuck you?" he threatens. His free hand caresses between my cleavage, and it makes me feel sick.

"What the hell are you doing, Roc?" Alex booms. His entry into the room is commanding. I thought Roc was the one in charge, but now I just don't know. For now, I'm glad he's here. Was Roc about to rape me? "Get the damn video recorder and let's get this shit done." *Wait what?* Roc eases off of me, but not before winking.

"Later," he mouths. He leaves the room, but returns two minutes later with some type of camcorder. For the first time, I see the newspaper in Alex's hand when he shoves it at me.

"Hold this with the date showing," he says dryly. I do as he says, waiting to see what they're going to do next. I look at the date and see that it has been exactly two days since I was taken from Grayson's house. I can't believe I was out of it that long. "Hold the paper at chest level and look into the recorder," Alex instructs. Again I comply and he starts the video. The recording goes on for a few minutes without a single word spoken. *Weird as shit.* No demands were made. Alex turns off the recorder and doesn't look in my direction was he exits the room.

Roc walks stealthily toward me with a huge smile on his face. "Now that he's gone, we can play a bit." He pulls me up from the chair and the paper I'm holding slips to the floor. Hell no, this is not happening without a fight. I begin to buck against him, but he just laughs. He drags me across the room and throws me onto the bed.

"Fuck you, cocksucker!" I scream. He climbs on top of me and pins my hands above my head with one hand. His other hand comes down hard against my cheek. Tears slide down my face, but I don't give him the pleasure of hearing the sobs escape my mouth. I squirm wildly, trying my best to buck him off of me. When his hand is close enough to my face, I bite the hell out of him. He grunts incoherently. That stunt earns me a punch to the gut. Air rushes out me and I can't breathe. The tears fall harder.

"You fucking little cunt. You're going to pay for that." As

he inspects his bitten hand, Alex walks back into the room. His eyebrows knit together in anger.

"Roc? What the hell, man?" Roc jumps off of me like a guilty person caught with their hand in the cookie jar.

"That little bitch just bit me," he explains.

"What were you doing? From the looks of things, you were trying to have sex with her," Alex huffs. "I'm not into rape, Roc. I didn't sign up for this shit. We do the ransom, get the money, and that is it. I won't be a part of anything else or have it on my conscious that I let it happen in my presence."

"Well, it wouldn't be in your presence if you'd stop coming to her damn rescue," Roc argues. "I was just having a little fun. Nobody asked you to participate. Don't act all holier than thou. You're just as much a part of this kidnapping as I am." During the midst of their argument my eyes are drawn to Roc's right hand that he is rubbing from my bite—specifically the tattoo. *That freaking scorpion tattoo.* Oh God! How did I not make this connection before.

"It's you," I accuse, pointing at Roc. "You were the pizza delivery guy who came to my house a couple of weeks ago. I remember the tattoo now." He had on a cap that day, but I can't say that I paid enough attention to him to notice. I was too busy trying to tip him so I could get him out. He creeped me out then and I didn't pay attention to my instincts. I was distracted by Liam's unannounced visit. The grin Roc is sporting right now tells me that I'm right. It was him.

"Kind of slow there, doll," he chuckles.

"Just stay the hell away from her," Alex warns, bringing the conversation back to Roc's attempt to rape me. "Say what you want, but I will not let you harm her while I'm here. I can't have that shit on my conscious too. You don't have to like it, but you will respect it."

"Whatever," Roc replies dismissively. "Oh and if that douche bag wouldn't have been there that day, I would've taken you then. You were almost too easy. When I did come back for you, this one was with me," he says pointing over at Alex. "So don't let his white cape fool you, he wants this money just as much as I do. He won't give a shit what happens to you after he gets it and I'll be waiting." He laughs as he walks out of the door. My heart drops because I know that he is right. I try to scoot back further on the bed as Alex walks toward me and a pain shoots through my stomach where Roc punched me. I bend over to hide my face.

"Are you hurt?" he asks.

"I'm fine," I lie.

"Siobhan, look at me." I would ask how he knows my name again, but of course he does. Those fuckers were watching my every move. I don't look up or answer him. Let my silence give him a hint that he can fuck off too. "I'm not going to hurt you and I'm not going to let anyone else hurt you, either."

As a reflex, my head whips up at that statement. I stare him coldly in the eyes. *Really motherfucker because I'm already hurting from the blow your jackass partner delivered right before you came in.* "Really," I answer sarcastically.

"Shit, your face, it's all red." He flinches. He moves my hair away from my right cheek and I jump. "Roc fucking hit you." He looks down and sees that I'm guarding my stomach. He snatches my shirt up to get a look before I can protest. "God damn it." He gets up and begins to pace. He then leaves the room and closes the door behind him.

I can hear him arguing with Roc downstairs, but the actual words are not intelligible. I strain to hear, but it is no use. Wait, I didn't hear Alex put the locks on the door after he left. I can make a run for it. I desperately try to remember the route I was taken on to get to this room when I had that damn pillow case on my head. How can I get past them without being seen? Maybe If I can just escape to a room that has a phone, I can call 9-1-1. Yes, that sounds more feasible. Once they ping my location, they can send help. I won't have to try to get away. Just as I try to set this plan in motion, Alex comes back in carrying two ice packs. Roc's words about me being slow mock me.

"Here. One pack is for your face and the other is for your stomach. This won't happen again. He won't be back in here without me." He sets the ice packs next to me on the bed and walks back out. This time I do hear him locking the door from the other side. I count them. There are three clicks. So much for that plan. I will just have to be more attentive. The next time that door is left unlocked, I need to be ready to act. I need to figure out a way to save myself before they get what they want from this.

The silence is deafening. The house is quiet now and I'm left alone with my thoughts. The ice that I'm using on my face and stomach is the only thing that is keeping me grounded in the here and now. I wish this was just a really bad dream. I wonder how my family is dealing with all of this. How Jordan and Grayson are holding up. A tear escapes as I think about my last memory of Grayson having Vanessa at his house. Our break up had crushed me. Still I know he must be worried.

Vanessa is probably glad to have me out the picture. *Bitch.* The thought that this may be how it all ends terrifies me. Roc's words about Alex not caring once he gets the money replay in my mind. He promised to be waiting for that moment. Was that his way of saying that he is going to finish what he started, before he kills me? This is the type of shit you see on soap operas or some television drama. Hard to believe this is my reality right now. My parents have some money put away, but they're not rich.

A light bulb suddenly goes off. Grayson is fucking ridiculously rich. They're going to try to get the ransom from him. This was probably the plan all along and I stupidly kept him in the dark about it all. He is going to be blindsided. If I had just told him, maybe he could have used his connections to catch these fuckers before they took me. Instead, I trusted that Officer Richards would find out who was behind the calls. I let my guard down once the calls stopped. I just figured whoever it was grew bored with me. I had no idea a bigger plan had been put into place or that there were two of them. Alex seems like he is just in it for the money and truly wants to keep me safe in this. Roc is the evil one. If it is up to him, I know he won't let me go. I don't even know if this ransom scheme is bigger than just the two of them. Either way, I know I need to save myself.

Chapter 2

I guess at some point I fell asleep, although I have no sense of time—whether it's morning or evening. I'm lying in a wet spot from the melted ice. I shove the ice packs aside and sit up. I wince at the soreness in my stomach. I never did turn the light off in the room so my eyes work to acclimate while I rub them. Once they can focus, I notice a brown envelope near the door. The Hamburger Helper that Alex brought to me last night is still sitting in the chair because I was too upset to eat. My stomach growls, but I'm too focused on the envelope that now has my full attention. I ease out of bed and take timid steps toward it. As I pick up the envelop, I read the words "Enjoy" written with a black Sharpie. Butterflies flutter in my belly and my heart quickens. Somehow, I know this isn't good. My fingers tremble as I bend back the clasps that will unleash whatever contents await me. It's photographs—8x10, black and white photographs. I see the first photo and I drop the whole lot. *What the fuck?*

The photos are of Grayson and Vanessa. In one photo, he is unzipping the back of her dress. In another photo, he is closing the curtains. There are various photos of them at some sort of cafe, museum, and wait—what? The fucking Eiffel Tower. They're in Paris. The place he was supposed to take me after graduation. A piece of paper sticks out between them so I pick it up. *'Taken a few days ago. Thought you may want to see how much the professor is missing you'.*

My whole world shatters. Grayson is in Paris while I'm

being held captive. How can this be real? The photos don't look photoshopped. If he is in Paris, does even know I'm missing? What if he left before Jordan could tell him and she can't get through to him. This makes no sense. Surely, he would have seen my car in his driveway. Maybe he just ignored it. I sink to the floor and pick up each individual photo, committing them all to memory. I will never forgive him for this, either way. If it is so easy for him to move on with Vanessa, then we don't belong together. Surely he can't know that I'm missing. He isn't that heartless. That is beside the point though. It doesn't make me feel any better. One sob wracks my body before I commence into a full on ugly cry. The harder I cry, the louder I get. I can't help it. I've held strong until this point, but now the damn has broken. I'm pretty sure this little gift came from Roc. He wins. If his plan was to break me, then mission accomplished.

I hear the locks turning, but I can't bring myself to move or care. Alex walks in and just stands over me looking at all of the photos. "Motherfucker," he mumbles. He kneels down and pushes a bowl of oatmeal toward me. He then begins scooping up all the photos and stuffing them back into the envelope. "Ignore this shit," he suggests.

"So, they're real?" I want so desperately for him to tell me no—that it's just some sick joke that Roc has come up with.

"Yeah, they're real. Roc is a dick for showing these to you. Just stay strong. This is almost over."

"And that is supposed to make me feel better. Don't you think I've already figured out what will happen to me once this is over," I sniff.

"You're going to make it out of here, that's what. Look, I can't tell you shit, but just trust me. I know you don't have a reason to, but just try. Okay?" There's a glimpse of sincerity in his eyes, almost convincing.

"Does Grayson know that I'm missing?" I challenge.

"Yes. Now that is all that I can tell you. Don't let Roc get under your skin. Wait until you get out of here and seek answers for yourself. Now eat before you make yourself sick." He puts the last photo in the envelope, grabs the old bowl of food from the chair and heads out the door. I'm left sitting on the floor, sniffling and trying to decode his message. So Grayson does know. Did he find out before or after his little impromptu trip to Paris with that bitch? At least I know that my original theory was right. They're trying to shake him down for the money. Question is, am I worth it to him? Just how dispensable am I? I know these are toxic thoughts, but it is the way I feel right now. Hurt and anger battle within for the dominant emotion over this whole situation. I still can't get over the fact he took her to Paris. The one place on earth that is my dream come true.

Hell, he could have taken her to Italy…anywhere, but Paris. This feels intentional and like a big 'fuck you'. He had to know that I'd find out, even if I hadn't been taken. I push the bowl of oatmeal aside and crawl back to the bed. I curl into a ball. I don't even give a shit that my stomach is protesting in pain and hunger. I want the darkness, damn it. I don't want to feel this. I cry until sleep finally has mercy on me and takes me under.

* * *

"Siobhan…Siobhan? I need you to wake up." A woman's voice wakes me from my slumber. I rub my eyes and turn toward the voice. At first glance, I'm caught off guard. She has long red hair like mine, but with green eyes. The similarities are astounding. We could probably pass for sisters the resemblance is so strong. Oh God…am I already dead and my angel is here to take me? The light nudge this woman gives as she calls my name a third time, wakes me from my semi consciousness. Well if she isn't an angel, has she come to save me or is she with the other two?

"Who are you?" I ask groggily. Please be here to rescue me. Something tells me she isn't, but I can hope.

"My name is Celine," she says wrinkling her nose. I raise my arm and sniff. Yup, it's me. I stink. I haven't been allowed to shower since I've been here and I've been wearing the same clothes since they've taken me. "Yes, you do smell, but hopefully we can get you home today," she confirms.

"So you're working with Alex and Roc?" Shock registers on her face that I know the names of the other two kidnappers.

"I don't work with anyone. We're all here for the same purpose—yes. Today is the drop so it is important that you do everything that you're told so that nobody gets hurt." Celine looks me in the eye, waiting for my reply. "Do you understand? No funny business."

"Fine. I just want to get out of here alive," I quip.

"I want that too. Come on, they're waiting for us downstairs. I'm going to have ask you to put this over your head." It's that damn pillow case again. I hate that freaking thing, but I don't want a repeat of my forced compliance. I stand up and do as she says. After the pillow case is over my head, she begins to lead me out the door. I take each step carefully, my hands steadily searching for something to hold on to. There is nothing. Celine puts one of my hands on her shoulder to help lead me. When we get down stairs, the change in temperature, and the slight breeze, alert me that we're now outside. I'm helped into what I'm guessing is van due to the vastness of the space, before my wrists are tied to something behind me. The material feels like rope and is digging into my skin tightly. The pillow case is left over my head. I know squirming will only make it worse so I try to focus on something else—like, I may actually be set free.

I hear the door finally slam. The van rumbles to life. I strain to make out the voices in the distance, but I can also feel breathing in close proximity. Someone is back here with me. I stay quiet and work to stay upright with each bump of the road. I'm sitting on the floor with my legs straight out in front of me and my arms tied behind me so my balance is already off. The ride seems to go on forever. My nerves are on edge with each mile we drive. Celine said today was the drop. I'm guessing that was code for the exchange—me for the money. Are they really going to let me go? Are they really going to let Grayson walk away? Shit, is he the one making the drop? They will probably kill us both. I can't help but be pessimistic. I hope he has a plan…like the FBI waiting to get these motherfuckers. I may not forgive him for being with Vanessa in Paris, but I don't want him to die trying to save me either.

These possible scenarios are driving me crazy. I'm so freaking scared, yet I want this all to be over. After what seems like hours, we finally come to a stop. I hear two doors close on the van—driver and passenger. I wait a few minutes, but the door to where I am remains closed. I try to shake the pillow case loose from my head, but it is futile.

"Stay still, Siobhan. This is almost over," a male voice says lightly. It's Alex. I knew I wasn't back here alone. I could feel his presence.

"When? How long before you let me go?" I want to keep him talking.

"Soon. Just do exactly what you're told. They will be coming for you any minute now." I hate that his answers are so vague.

"Can you take this pillow case off my head at least?" I ask. The damn thing is just making me more anxious.

"Not yet. It's almost over," he repeats. "Try to stay calm." I guess he can sense that I'm silently freaking the fuck out. My adrenaline is in overdrive. Fight or flight has kicked in. Just as Alex promised, the van door slides open. They're here for me. I can feel someone grab my arm to assist me out after untying me from whatever they had me shackled to, but the pillowcase and restraints remain in place. "Remember what I said," Alex says from behind me.

The grip tightens on my bicep and I almost holler out in pain. "No talking or funny shit when I pull this thing off your head," Roc warns. I'd know his evil voice anywhere. It drips with disdain for me.

"Shut the hell up, Roc." That is Celine. I didn't know she was with us. So both Alex and Celine are walking with us. That makes me feel a little better. I don't trust Roc. "Let's hurry up and get this done so we can get the hell away from here."

We walk a little more before finally coming to stop. "Let me see her." Oh God. It is Grayson. He's here. Roc abruptly pulls the pillow case from over my head, but not before I feel the cold metal of his gun in my back. We're in a huge, empty warehouse. My eyes immediately zoom in on Grayson standing there with two large duffel bags on each side of him. He's alone and he has some muscle head looking guy with a gun aimed at him. I hope he has back up waiting for the word to swoop in. If not, we're both fucked. I can't get a read on Grayson. With his flat affect, I could be a stranger...this could be a routine business transaction. He doesn't look like a man worried about a gun being aimed at him or distraught that someone he loves is being held captive.

"Celine, go over and get the bags from him." Alex instructs. "We need to make sure all the money is there." Celine nods and walks over to Grayson. I see something pass over his face briefly, but it is gone in a flash. It was the tiniest of reactions, but I saw it. It was a break in his mask, but now it's gone. He hands Celine the first bag and she brings it back and sets it on the ground next to Alex's feet before retrieving the other bag. Alex kneels down to unzip them both. *Holy shit that is a lot of money.* The bag is filled with wads of money banded together with mustard colored straps that have $10,000 written on them. Roc actually loosens his grip to get a closer look.

"Is it all there?" Roc asks.

"How in hell do you think I can count five million that fast?" Alex replies sarcastically. He flips through the money bands. "I making sure that there aren't any dye packs in here and that the entire stack is made up of hundreds and not blank paper."

"Celine, make sure there are 250 stacks in that duffel while I count this one," Alex continues. Celine nods her head in understanding and they both count silently.

"I have 250," Celine confirms.

"Same here," Alex agrees. He stands and pulls a hidden gun from his hip. Celine follows suit. "Rick, go bring the van around. I have the money bags in my sight. He so much as flinches and I will cap his ass." The guy with the gun aimed at Grayson slowly lowers his weapon and begins to head in the direction of the van. So he was the driver. Now what? Where did sensible Alex go? What happens once the van is brought around?

"You know we can't just let them go Alex. That was never the plan. Bogdan gave the command to clean this up as soon as the deal was done. The FBI will be hot on our trail if they aren't already," Roc points out.

"We never discussed this. We were just supposed to get the score, collect our 300k, and go our separate ways. No mess. These would be capital murder charges we're facing."

"Only if we get caught. Bogdan isn't going to let that happen. They've seen our faces Alex. They know too much. Letting them go will only lead to us getting caught. You just get in the van with Celine and I'll clean this up with Rick."

"I agree," Celine says. I look over at Grayson, but he still appears emotionless. How can he remain so calm? This is the end of the road for us.

"Let's just hurry this shit up," Alex acquiesces. He briefly looks over at Celine and she nods. The next few seconds happen so quickly. Rick pulls up and gets out to help Roc 'clean up.' Celine quickly draws her gun and shoots him while Alex unloads multiple rounds into Roc. I drop to my knees and scream at the gunfire exchange going on around me. I close my eyes tightly as I hear Roc's body drop behind me. So Celine and Alex have gone rogue—probably to keep the five million for themselves. I keep waiting to feel the next bullet tear into my flesh.

The sound of voices screaming 'stay on the ground' and 'don't move' has me brave enough to open my eyes. Help is here. As I suspected, several FBI uniforms storm the warehouse. There are too many of them to count. Celine comes behind me and begins to untie the rope. Why aren't the FBI apprehending her and Alex.

"It's all over," she says. "I'm an FBI agent and so is Alex." *Holy shit!* Grayson is at my side in seconds.

"Oh, thank God, you're all right. I'm so sorry, baby, that this happened to you." I allow myself to get lost in his embrace for a moment before I pull back. I'm so grateful that he came for me, but it doesn't change the fact that he went to Paris with Vanessa. I won't be a bitch about it because I owe this man my gratitude, but the possibility for our reunion is no longer an option. Right now, I'm just glad that we're both safe. He takes one look at the redness of my cheek and growls.

"I'm fucking guessing the Roc guy did this," Grayson speculates as he caresses my cheek. "I wish I could kill that bastard for hurting you."

"I thought…"

"Tranquil shots to put them down. They're still alive and will answer for all the shit they've done," Alex fills in as he walks up.

"Did you know that Alex and Celine were FBI agents? You seemed so calm the whole time," I inquire. Grayson and Celine exchange glances.

"They told me they had someone on the inside, but I didn't know who. I just knew I had to play it cool so that I wouldn't tip their hand. Plus I knew we had back up waiting for the precise moment to swarm in." Grayson shakes Alex and Celine's hands and thanks them. He grabs me by the shoulders and pulls me into him. "Come on. Let me get you out of here. They'll have plenty of questions for you, but I told them I wanted to get you a bath, change of clothes, food, and some rest first." I sniff my clothes and wrinkle my nose. Ugh, yes I need a bath. After that, he and I are going to talk.

"Thank you for everything, Grayson. And yes, I'd appreciate a chance to regroup before I relive this nightmare." He gives me a tight squeeze.

Chapter 3

So it turns out that I've been in New York the entire time—held in an abandoned home off the beaten path. A private jet was used to transport my unconscious body thousands of miles away from home. I have so many questions. I refuse to go anywhere looking like this so Grayson is taking us to his residence at the Waldorf Astoria. Of course he would have a place here in New York. The expanse of how far this man's money reaches doesn't surprise me anymore. When we arrive in valet, the attendant arches a brow in question when he sees me, but quickly recovers. I know I look like shit. I'm sure more curious stares will be directed at me so I'm careful to keep my head down as we make our way inside toward the elevators. We stop at the 42nd floor for the penthouse suite.

"Do you have a taste for anything in particular? I can get you a menu," Grayson offers.

"It doesn't really matter. A burger will be fine—just a plain ole burger." His home is as gorgeous as I expected. The Italian decor is breathtaking, but something still feels off. I'm a ball of nerves right now. We have so much unsettled history between us that needs to be resolved.

"That will be easy enough. I'll get that ordered for you and then I'll draw you a bath." Grayson disappears around the corner and I walk into the living room. I don't want to have a seat because I don't want to soil his expensive furniture.

The burger arrives within twenty minutes and of course it is gourmet and comes with a mountain of fries. I'm sure they don't have anything regular here. While Grayson tips the delivery guy, I take the food into the dining room. I reluctantly have a seat. I feel so dirty. Grayson follows me and sits across from me.

"What's wrong, Siobhan? You've been awfully quiet." The absence of my nickname tells me that my mood change hasn't gone unnoticed.

"We need to talk," I say, taking a deep breath. "We can't pretend things didn't end the way they did." Grayson runs his hands through his hair as I pick at my burger.

"Baby, I didn't mean any of it. The office blow up, the club—none of it. It was all for show. The dean gave you implicit instructions to stay away from me and you were rebelling against them. And for what? I couldn't let you ruin your academic future." I sit up straighter in my chair. Fury unleashes within me as the memories from my conversation with the dean flood my mind.

"Nobody told you to take the fall for me Grayson. As a matter of fact, I remember specifically asking you not to. That is why I came to see you." I push the plate of food away from me. "How am I supposed to feel, knowing I cost you your job?" He snickers a little and I swear I want to slap him. This isn't funny.

"Shiv, I didn't lose my job. I simply agreed to take the remainder of the semester off to draw attention away from the rumors on campus. The university didn't want a scandal and neither did I. The dean agreed that if I stayed away from you, he wouldn't bring about any academic punishment for you. Those were the terms. My family donates too much money to that school for my job to be threatened."

"Okay, well what about Vanessa?" I accuse.

"What about her?" he retorts.

"Don't play stupid, Grayson," I huff. "The day I got taken, I was there to see you and she was there. You took her to Paris, for God's sake. Paris, Grayson—my place. Yes, that scumbag Roc guy showed me the pictures." I watch as the color drains from his face.

"Paris wasn't my idea, but I had to go. That was originally my father's business trip. The Feds thought it was important that I go to show those fuckwads that they hadn't broken me. I was portraying the ruthless business man to keep them from having me jump through hoops. Any weakness on my part would have been detrimental. Vanessa was part of that ploy." He runs his hands through his hair again, like he does when he is nervous. "Every move was calculated baby—the commercial flight so they could track me, the posing with Vanessa—everything!"

"That really hurt me," I reply as I look down. What he's telling me makes sense, but the pain is still here.

I know that he is telling me the truth, but I still hate that Vanessa got to go to Paris with him. "I believe you. I just need time to process it all." He gets up and comes to stand in front of me. He lifts my chin and I'm forced to see the hurt in his eyes staring back at me.

"What about you baby? Why didn't you tell me what was going on? The car accident, the phone calls—you kept me in the dark about it all. I could have helped you. We probably could have prevented all of this." He pulls me into his chest and rests his chin on top of my head. "I was so mad at you for keeping that from me, but I'm just glad you're safe."

"I thought about telling you, but I didn't want you to worry. I had Officer Richards looking into it. Besides the calls stopped."

"That asshat needs to hand in his badge. His investigative skills suck, at best." Grayson shakes his head. "The feds were able to work with Jordan and the local police department to fit the pieces together. The calls to you stopped right around the time they started harassing me. I didn't mention it to you because I thought it was business related. This is why I couldn't stay mad at you. We both were guilty of keeping things from each other to spare worry. We just need to make sure from here on out, we always communicate."

"Okay," I agree. I'm done trying to find reasons to stay away from him. I look up at him and he kisses me softly on the lips. One thought crosses my mind, though, and I can't move on until I know. "Grayson, how did you find me? I know you said the FBI had people inside, but how did they do that?"

"The man that took you was the nephew of a Russian mob boss. The FBI already had two people deep undercover collecting evidence of money laundering, drug trafficking, murder, prostitution rings, and more. When you were taken, their undercover people found a way to reach out to see who had reported you missing. From there, a plan was made to get you back." Grayson wraps a strand of my hair around his finger. "We have to meet with their undercover team tomorrow and provide a debriefing. After that we will fly you home. Your family and mine are meeting for a late lunch, but for now let's just forget it all. Just be here with me." I nod in agreement.

"Okay," I say softly. I pick up my burger for a bite. I'm not really as hungry as I should be, but I know that I need to eat.

"I'm going to run you a bath. Stay here and finish your food." He winks at me and I give him a small smile. I don't know how I feel about lunch with his parents. I recall how the last visit with them went so, I'm hoping to avoid a repeat performance. Tomorrow will definitely be a challenging day. Reliving all that has tormented me.

* * *

The scent of lavender that wafts from the tub brings back the good memories. This is my thoughtful, romantic Grayson. I stand in the bathroom doorway and he motions for me to come in. As he turns to shut off the water, I quickly remove the clothes that I've been wearing for days. I never want to see them again. They can be burned for all I care. When I'm completely undressed, my hands cover my girly bits the best they can. It's been a while since I've been naked for him. A smile creeps across his lips, but he doesn't acknowledge the reappearance of my shyness. Instead he gets up, grabs my hand, and walk me the rest of the way to the tub. He helps me into the tub and I'm happy to be submerged within the silky water and bubbles.

"Relax, baby," he encourages. I lean back and he begins to wet my hair. It isn't until he applies some lavender shampoo to my hair, that I realize he is going to wash my hair. I guess lavender is the theme of this pampering tonight. I close my eyes as his nimble fingers massage my scalp. In this moment, nothing else matters. All the bad that we have experienced dissipates into a distant memory. I want the slate to be clean. I trust him when he says he is not involved with Vanessa and that everything that occurred leading up to, and after, my disappearance was all an act—for my benefit.

He rinses my hair, with an attachment that he connected to the faucet, and a moan slips past my lips. The water pressure on my scalp feels amazing. Grayson's hands pause and I giggle. He moves on to bathing me with a sponge but the attention he is paying to my breasts lets me know just how affected he is. I should have the cleanest breasts in the world.

"I think they're clean now, Grayson," I say in reference to the girls.

"*Hmmm*, let me check," he offers. He leans down over the tub and takes a nipple into his mouth. I'm stunned for a second, but then I melt into him. There is an instant tingle down below that gets me worked up. It has been far too long. My whimpers are the only encouragement he needs. He swirls his tongue around my nipple, before switching to the other one. He has me squirming within seconds. When he steps back to remove his clothes in a frenzy, I know that shit is about to get real. He gets into the tub with me and water sloshes everywhere. I try to lean forward, but he stands me up and takes the place where I was just sitting. He then pulls me down so that I'm straddling his lap. The look in his eyes is devious. I miss this. "Lift up, baby," he prompts.

I know what he is really telling me so I lift up and insert his already hard cock at my entrance. I'm so wet for him that no priming is needed.

I ease down on his length and I can't help but bite my lip on the way down. He fills me completely and it feels so damn good.

"Shit," I moan. "God, Grayson," are the only syllables I can get out.

"That's right. Take it all. Take what belongs to you." Grayson bounces me up and down on his dick, but the pace is too slow. I'm so hungry for this man that I just can't get enough. I tighten my grip on his outer thighs to stabilize my balance in the slippery water, before I slam back down on his cock. I set a rhythm that is chaotic and desperate for release. "Fuck me, Siobhan," he encourages with a wicked grin. He continues his assault on my nipples and I swear I'm about to explode already. His hands caress my back and the altering sensations has me on the brink of sensory overload. So gentle and romantic, yet this is pure fucking—make up for lost time fucking. My legs begin to quiver as the build up begins again. My grip on his thighs with my knees is slipping. Grayson doesn't miss a beat. His hands snake down to my hips and he keeps us on the rhythm I have set.

"I'm almost thereeeee…" I scream.

"Get there because I'm right there on the edge with you," he admits. He slams me down one more time and I lose it. I come all over him with the force of a tidal wave. He lets out his own groan before falling over the edge with me. I can feel him throbbing as I milk every ounce of cum from him. My legs shake with aftershock as we both work to come back from that fucktastic release.

"So it looks like I've gotten you all dirty again," Grayson says while smiling.

"It's okay. I like your kind of dirty," I tease. I remain in his embrace. Neither one of us seems like we want to be the first to let go. I can already feel him growing hard again. I snicker and he smacks my ass.

"See what happens when I go so long without having you? You make me insatiable." He rubs the spot he just smacked. "Let's take this to the bedroom. I'm far from done with you. Tonight we'll fuck, make love, and then fuck again. I want to do all the depraved shit to you that I know we've both been missing." I stand up and let the water drain off my body. Any momentary shyness has taken a back seat to my lust. I watch as his pupils dilate while he looks me up and down before standing up with me. He tilts my head back and captures my lips for the deepest kiss to date. Our tongues meet for a slow, sensual tango that communicates our love without words. God, how I've missed this man.

He breaks the kiss and is the first to get out of the tub. He instructs me to stay put while he dries off. He then gets another towel and motions for me to lean toward him. He scoops me out of the tub and into his arms in a cradle like position. He dries me off a bit before placing me on my feet to finish the job.

We don't bother with clothes. We simply walk to the bedroom hand in hand. The room is dimly lit with candles—more lavender fragrance permeates the air. Grayson must have prepared all of this while he ran my bath and I was nibbling at my burger. He is so good with details and creating a romantic ambiance. He picks up a remote from the nightstand and with a click, Ed Sheeran's *Kiss Me* begins to play. He never lets go of my hand though. I'm ready for him to kiss me again, but surprisingly I'm thrown onto the bed on my back.

"First, we fuck," he says by way of explanation. Grayson crawls up the length of my body before his hands firmly grip my thighs. "Wrap your legs around me baby."

I don't hesitate to follow his command. "Yes, Grayson," I say as my heads falls back onto the bed. I'm his for the taking. He uses one hand to stroke me and finds that I'm already soaking wet with anticipation. The shadows dance across his handsome features as the candles flicker. Within seconds, I feel his rock hard cock nudging my folds teasingly before it rests at my opening. I squirm in frustration. I need him in me now. And oh, does he deliver. He slams into me and I can't hold back the scream that leaves my body—not from pain, but from the most exquisite pleasure. "Fuck yeah," I encourage, as my hips gyrate to take more of his length.

"Hmmm, this pussy is greedy tonight. Good because, I plan on worshipping it thoroughly," Grayson promises. His voice is full of lust. It is so fucking sexy. He wraps his hand around my hair and gives it a slight tug as he drives into me. I'm so lost. The delicious bite of each of his strokes is almost too much to handle. I match his punishing rhythm until stars explode behind my eyes.

"Grrrrrraaaayson!" A few more thrusts and I feel the telltale throb of him coming with me. He bites my shoulder as he groans out his release. This is new, but the pain is not unbearable. Quite the opposite. I welcome it into our repertoire of kink. As promised, Grayson brings me to the most fantastic orgasms at least four more times before we both fall asleep from exhaustion.

Acknowledgements

First, we would like to thank our readers. Creed of Redemption exists because of you. Your support has been inspiring and is greatly appreciated. Next we want to thank Allan Spiers (Allan Spiers Photography), Sommer Stein (Perfect Pear Creative Covers), Vanessa Leret Bridges (PREMA Editing), Stacey Blake (Champagne Formats), Kylie Dermott (Give Me Books) for their critical eyes, encouragement, creativity, and incredible talent. They each played a vital role in making Creed of Redemption the best it could be. A big thanks goes to all the blogs who participated in the blog tour and release day blitz. Last, but certainly not least, we want to thank our personal assistants, Lauren Weber and Renee McKinney for keeping us organized as well as Christina Stanton and Heather Coker for their fill in assistance. We also want to thank all our Devious Divas members (Annette Elens, Jacquie Denison, Michelle Louise Drew, Rhiannon King, Alison Phillips, Chantel Pentz McKinley, Brandy Raub, and Stacey Louise) for their kick ass pimping and all of our Back Stage Pass groupies' support.

ABOUT THE
Authors

S.R. Watson

S.R. Watson is a Texas native who resides in Wisconsin. She is an operating room registered nurse who has evolved into an author of Erotica and Romantic Suspense. She grew up reading the Sweet Valley Series (Twins, High, & University) among others. Back then she would use notebook paper to create stories and cut pictures out of her mother's JC Penney catalogs for the characters she wanted to portray. She ventured away from reading and writing stories when she left home for college to pursue her BSN and then MBA, but picked up reading again in 2012. Her love for the stories written by her favorite authors made her decide to pursue own dreams of writing. Her Forbidden Trilogy was her debut release. Since then she has written the stand alone, The Object of His Desire, as well as co-written the start of the S.I.N. Rock Star Trilogy and The Adulteress, along side Shawn Dawson. She looks forward to sharing her writing journey with everyone.

When S.R. Watson is not writing, she likes to spend time with her family, read, listen to various genres of music, make hand-made natural soap, and travel. She is down to earth, loves a nice glass of wine, and is addicted to watching the television series Scandal.

SHAWN DAWSON

Shawn Dawson is an Illinois native who resides in Hampshire. He has always been an athlete, which has led to many achievements. He is currently a sponsored athlete for Fit Hustle. He is also a published cover model for sixteen books with more to release. His newest journey has taken him on a different path to pursue writing. He made his debut as an author along side S.R. Watson with Sex in Numbers; book one in the S.I.N. Rock Star Trilogy. He has also co-written the start of a six-book serial titled, The Adulteress Infidelity Chronicles. More books are in the works.

Shawn enjoys spending time with his daughter Mya and his fur babies, Camden and Rebel. He als o streams from both Xbox and PS4 (Destiny) so be sure to check him out at www.twitch.tv/theeshawndawson.

When Shawn is not writing, he also dedicates his time to working out and helping to change the lives of his online clients through coaching. Visit his page to find a nutrition / work out plan that right for you at www.dawsonteam.com

Other Books

S.I.N. Rockstar Trilogy
Sex in Numbers

Infidelity Chronicles
The Adultress

By S.R. Watson

The Forbidden Trilogy
Forbidden Attraction
Forbidden Love

The Object of His Desire

43413674R00135

Made in the USA
Middletown, DE
09 May 2017